Step-Chain

All over the country children go to stay with step-parents, stepbrothers and stepsisters at the weekends. It's just like an endless chain. A step-chain. *Don't Tell Mum* is the seventh link in this step-chain.

I'm Bethany. My best friend, Claire, is desperate for me to fancy someone. She thinks I'll like Robby, the good-looking waiter in Ric's café. And she's right. I do. But once I get to know Robby, I discover the truth about him. So now I'm under mega great mountains of pressure, because I can't tell Mum his secret. I can't tell anyone . . .

Collect the links in the step-chain! You never know who you'll meet on the way . . .

Step-Chain

DON'T TELL MUM

Ann Bryant

EGMONT

For the Cranstoun family – my great friends,
Sue, Ian, Katie and Naomi – with lots of love.

First published in Great Britain 2002
by Egmont Books Limited
239 Kensington High Street
London W8 6SA

Copyright © 2002 Ann Bryant
Series conceived and created by Ann Bryant
Cover illustration copyright © 2002 Mark Oliver

The moral rights of the author and cover illustrator have
been asserted

Series editor: Anne Finnis

ISBN 0 7497 4917 2

1 3 5 7 9 10 8 6 4 2

Typeset by Avon DataSet Ltd, Bidford on Avon, B50 4JH
(www.avondataset.co.uk)
Printed and bound in Great Britain by
Cox & Wyman Ltd, Reading, Berkshire

CONTENTS

Step-Chain

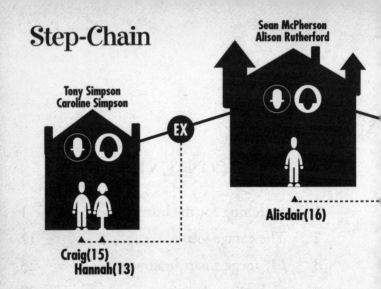

Sean McPherson
Alison Rutherford

Tony Simpson
Caroline Simpson

EX

Alisdair(16)

Craig(15)
Hannah(13)

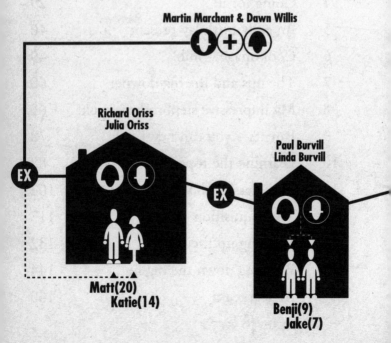

Martin Marchant & Dawn Willis

Richard Oriss
Julia Oriss

Paul Burvill
Linda Burvill

EX

EX

Matt(20)
Katie(14)

Benji(9)
Jake(7)

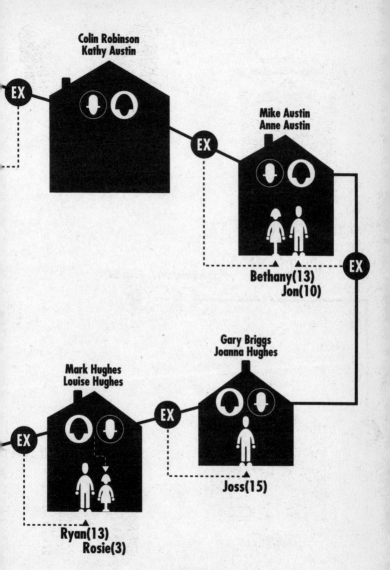

Colin Robinson
Kathy Austin

Mike Austin
Anne Austin

Bethany(13)
Jon(10)

Gary Briggs
Joanna Hughes

Mark Hughes
Louise Hughes

Joss(15)

Ryan(13)
Rosie(3)

Read on to discover all the links . . .

1 SEARCHING FOR THE BUZZ

I was walking into town at the end of another scintillating day at school, and talking to myself, like you do. Well, *I* do, anyway. I know some people think I'm completely barmy, but then I'm sure there must be others who think it's all part of my endearing character. I don't care what anyone thinks at the moment, because I've got to keep gabbling away to sort things out.

It's not fair. I mean, of all the people in the world, how come *I'm* the one to be staggering around under these mega great mountains of pressure? I mean, all I want is one little Coke in Ricoco's café so I can suss out this boy who works there. My best friend, Claire, has been on about him for days. 'You're going to absolutely love him,' she keeps telling me at school. 'He's sooo good looking.'

'So why don't *you* fancy him then?' I wanted to know.

'Because he's not my type. He's too nice and neat and normal . . . and he goes red easily.'

And that's when I realised that he probably wasn't that good looking at all. Claire's just desperate for me to fancy someone – anyone – so we'll both be in the same boat. I've never fancied any ordinary people – only pop stars, whereas Claire's spent the last year fancying one boy after another. At the moment it's the boy who works on the checkout at the supermarket. She keeps telling me what a great feeling it is.

'Your whole body buzzes like crazy, Beth!' I keep wondering when *my* body might show some sign of buzzing like crazy, but so far, no luck.

Back to the mega tonnes of pressure. Last night Anne, my stepmother – and don't get me wrong, I love her dearly – said I was to come straight home after school because (1) I haven't got any money (that's true), (2) I'm behind with my homework (also sadly true) and (3) I'm doing far too much gadding about these days. Now that last one is blatantly untrue. At least, I think it is. It would help if I knew what 'gadding' meant, but I'm pretty sure I haven't been doing it.

Anyway, after Anne had passed sentence on the Coke at the café, I went to a great deal of trouble phoning Claire and whispering down the phone that she had to ring me back a subtle twenty minutes later, to remind me about a very important 'netball practice'. So far, so good. Or at least that's what I thought. But, stupidly, I hadn't taken into account that my adorable little stepbrother, Jon, might happen to be loitering outside my bedroom with his ear pressed to the door.

So when I came to tell Anne twenty minutes later that Claire had just phoned me and, silly me, I'd completely forgotten about the netball practice after school the next day, the earwig pipes up, 'She hasn't got a netball practice, 'cos I know.'

'I *have*!' I screeched, which was overdoing it slightly, I admit.

'She's just made it up so she can go to Ricoco's,' Jon informed Anne.

I resisted the urge to strangle him – some kind person really should have done that long ago to put the rest of us out of our misery – and told Anne that I was Goal Attack and they couldn't do without me. I trailed off into some sort of pleading jargon that covers all occasions when I'm desperate to get the parental OK as quickly as possible, then get off the subject.

'You know I don't mind you staying for netball practice, Bethany,' came the verdict, 'but I've already told you you're not to go to the café, and I'm trusting you not to.'

Uh-oh! Tough one. Anne knows exactly how to get me where it hurts. So there I was, stranded on the horns of a dilemma, which is as painful as it sounds, believe me.

But to make matters worse, Jon went ominously quiet after Anne had spoken, and right now I'm fearing the worst. So while I'm walking along talking to myself I'm looking to right and left, because something tells me that any minute now, smart-kid Jon is suddenly going to catch me out. I know exactly how his evil little mind works. First he will have got himself an invite to his friend Alex's house after school. Then he'll probably get Alex to cover for him while he nips down to the bottom of his garden, climbs over the wall, runs down the alleyway, and hey presto(!) into the high street. And guess where I am right now? Yep. The high street.

And what do you know? There he is! Grinning his stupid head off.

'What are *you* doing?' I snapped.

In my heart I knew I was on to a loser from the very start, but there was just one chance. I looked around for any sign of Alex's mum. Good, she was nowhere to be seen. I narrowed my eyes and spoke in my most teacherly voice. 'You'd better not be on your own or I'll tell Anne.'

I was kind of hoping MI5 boy's grin might disappear at the sound of those foreboding words. But no chance.

'You can tell Mum what you like, she won't be interested, because Alex's mum is only back there . . .' He flapped his hand behind him. I had no way of knowing if he was telling the truth or not, and no time to find out because he was going in for the kill. 'And *I* reckon Mum'll be more interested in what *I* tell her about you not being at netball.'

I so wished he wouldn't do that 'I' thing, where his voice goes all loud and clever.

'For all you know I might be just buying something like . . . a snack . . . for the netball practice . . .'

Well, those words had to be in with a chance of winning the Most-stupid-excuse-of-the-year trophy.

'You're going to Ricoco's. It's obvious,' he grinned. 'I won't tell Mum if you give me a pound. And I know you've got a pound because I saw it in your room.'

He also knew he'd got me cornered. And what's more, he knew *I* knew he'd got me. I decided not to waste any more time on the nauseating, grinning little tale-telling, black-mailing MI5 earwig.

'I'll give it you at the weekend. I can't go into Ric's with no money, can I?'

'It'll be *two* pounds at the weekend.'

My jaw was hanging open. I'd never imagined that Jon could be this mercenary. 'Who put you up to that? Best friend Alex?'

He shook his head violently. Good, he was acting a bit more like a ten-year-old now.

'Alex'd never say anything like that. Alex likes you. In fact –' the smile turned into an embarrassed giggle – 'he fancies you.'

I rolled my eyes to the sky, and spoke in a withering voice. 'Alex is nine, yes?' He nodded. 'And I'm thirteen going on fourteen, if you remember.'

I gave him a look that was supposed to show I was about as impressed by his latest revelation as I was by the fact that caterpillars eat leaves. Then I deliberately changed it into a deeply disappointed look, and spoke in a matching voice to try and make the evil little blackmailer crack.

'I can't believe that I've got such a horrible brother.' And with these words I reached into my pocket and held out the pound coin.

This was a big gamble. I was playing the guilt card, and it seemed to be working pretty well. He began to squirm as he looked at the coin.

'You can give me two at the weekend – I've told you.'

'I can't afford two. Take this one. I'll just have to have a few sips of Claire's Coke, that's all.'

'Where *is* Claire?' he asked, looking round.

'She's meeting me in there. She had to nip home for something first.'

The grin came back. 'I bet *I* know why. It's to get changed, isn't it? She's got a boyfriend, hasn't she? She wants to look all –'

He broke off abruptly, because guess who'd suddenly appeared? Claire. She was wearing hipster jeans, a tight black top and a denim jacket. Her long light brown hair hung exactly where it was supposed to hang, and she looked altogether brilliant. Standing next to her in my school uniform, I felt like a pathetic little girl.

Claire looked at the pound I was holding out. 'What's happening?' she asked brightly.

'Ask him,' I said, jerking my head in Jon's direction, feeling a little flutter of hope. Jon wouldn't want to show his horrible greed in front of my sophisticated friend with the shining hair, would he?

'Bethany owes me,' he tried to explain.

'Is that your last quid, Beth?'

I sighed and nodded.

'You'll have to pay him later,' said Claire. 'We need that quid for Ric's. I haven't got any money at all.' She turned to Jon as she dragged me away from him. 'Seeya.' Then she broke into an awkward run, still clutching me and my pound. 'He's *soooo* gorgeous, Beth!'

I turned my head sharply, because my mind was still on my stepbrother, and I thought Claire must have suddenly lost her marbles.

'The waiter at Ric's,' she explained, her eyes going gooey. 'Though not as nice as the boy at the supermarket,' she added.

Then we were there. At the café.

2 THE GARAGE JOB

'So where is he?' I asked the moment we'd got a table.

'Stop staring round, Beth!' said Claire. She was studying the menu as though it contained the winning numbers of next week's lottery roll over. 'You're making it too obvious that you're interested.'

'But I *am* interested.' I stared round even more. The café was very busy and noisy. There were three waitresses rushing round, but no sign of any waiters at all, let alone boy wonder waiters.

I drummed my fingers on the table. 'Are you sure you didn't imagine him?'

'No,' hissed Claire, bringing the menu a couple of centimetres closer to her face.

And at that moment, out of the kitchen came a really good-looking boy. My jaw must have been hanging open or something because Claire sat up straight.

'Is it him?' she squeaked, keeping her eyes fixed on the menu.

'Well, he's just come out of the kitchen, so I'm guessing yes.'

'But are you sure it's him?'

'No, not totally. Maybe he just likes wearing aprons.'

And then he was standing there, pen poised, and I got the chance to look at him properly. My entire insides squeezed together, and for the first time in my life I was struck dumb. It must have shown because Claire kicked my ankle so hard I just knew there'd be a bruise there the next day. I guessed he was sixteen, about two metres tall with short dark hair, cut so it stuck up in soft spikes.

'Are you ready to order?'

He'd got a bit of an accent, but I wasn't sure what it was. Or maybe it wasn't an accent – maybe it was just his way of talking. Then I noticed that he'd gone rather pink – so this was what Claire meant. But I wouldn't have minded if he'd gone beetroot red, I was so hooked.

'Er . . . I'll have a Coke, please,' said Claire, in a strange voice that she didn't normally use.

As he jotted it down I took a quick sideways glance at Claire and saw that she was trying not to giggle.

'Anything else?' he asked me.

Great! Claire had made me look a right idiot, and yet I was the one with the pound coin. I was going to kill her. Meanwhile, I had to try and get my vocal cords to work. 'N-no, thanks.'

'You see what I mean, don't you?' Claire gushed, the moment he'd gone. 'Isn't he gorgeous?'

I could only nod. My whole body was zinging and my head felt as though it was inside out, with my mind on view for everyone to see my brilliant new feelings. And for the first time ever I felt a little touch of jealousy, because all the time Claire was sitting there with her stomach showing, her shiny lips pouting and her earrings swinging, there was no chance that he would look at me.

'You're blushing like mad, Beth!' said Claire. Then she giggled. 'That's something you've got in common already! I knew you'd fancy him. Isn't it brilliant?'

I nodded again. Then we both giggled again. But a couple of seconds later Claire's eyes clouded over. 'Look, that girl over there obviously fancies him too.'

One look at the competition at the other end of the café, and I knew I was way down the list.

'Did you hear that, Beth? She called him Robby. Right. When he brings my Coke, I'll say, "Oh sorry, it's for Bethany actually," then when he puts it in front of you, you say, "Cheers, Robby." And make sure you look sexy, OK? You have to tip your head on one side and stick your lips out a bit. That's what it says in my magazine, anyway.'

I really wanted a practice, but there was no time, because he was suddenly right there. My heart thudded noisily as he put the Coke down in front of Claire.

'Oh sorry, it's for Bethany actually.'

This was it! I pushed my lips forwards and tipped my head on one side. 'Cheers, Robby . . .' I drooled.

He gave me a sharp little nod, as if to say, 'Thanks for the thanks,' then he went.

'Wicked, Beth!' said Claire a second later. 'He smiled. He definitely smiled. I'm sure he likes you. Next time we come here, you've got to get changed first, OK?'

I'd already decided that.

Jon roared into my room the moment he was back from Alex's.

'You've got to give me that two pounds, you know, otherwise I'm telling.'

I flapped my hand to get him out of my room. 'Yeah, yeah . . .'

'Promise?'

'Promise,' I said flatly.

But it wasn't good enough for Greedy Chops. He made me sign this grubby bit of paper, on which he'd written:

I, the hereby sined person underneaf, does promise to give her brother Jon Gareth

Briggs the sum of two pounds at this forth
coming weekend.
SIGNITCHER . . . .

And the moment I'd signed the thing, I realised
something seriously bad.

'I don't get pocket money. I'm on an
allowance now, aren't I? I get it monthly.'

'Well, you should have thought of that.'

'It's not my fault, is it?'

'When's the next time you get paid?'

'The Saturday after this one.'

'Well, that's no good. I'm telling!'

And with that he shot out of my room.

'OK, I'll earn it!' I screamed after him.

I was in the nick of time because he'd got as
far as the kitchen door. We met on the stairs
and spoke in spiky whispers.

'How are you going to earn it?'

'Doing jobs on Saturday morning.'

'Like what?'

'Washing the car, going to the shop for Anne . . . I dunno – anything.'

'Ask her right now then. Go on.'

Inside I was seething. How dare the little ten-year-old upstart wield such power. I was going to get him back for this one day.

Anne was ironing when I went into the kitchen. She was also watching some weepy film that she'd recorded, so the iron was moving very slowly indeed.

'You don't need to spray water on the clothes, do you?' I grinned. 'Just drip tears on to them!'

I thought that was a nice friendly jokey sort of opener, but Anne wasn't impressed.

'Sshh! This is the best bit!'

I went back to the door and mouthed to Jon, who was sitting on the stairs with a sneery look on his face, 'She's watching something. I'll ask later.'

Jon went cross-eyed, which is what he does to give me the idea that I'm the biggest dur in the world. But I was saved because Dad (*my* dad, Jon's stepdad) walked in at that moment.

'Hi, Beth!' he said, giving me a hug. Then he did his usual thing to Jon, which is to jump into a boxing pose, fists up, shoulders up, legs bent, as though he was all ready to throw a right-hander. Jon was clearly beginning to tire of this now. He managed a weak smile and even stood up and did the pose back. But it was no wonder he wasn't exactly grinning his head off. Dad had been doing this greeting for the last three years.

'Where's your mum, Jon?'

'Kitchen.'

'Dad?' I quickly stopped him before he entered the no-speaking zone. 'Have you got any jobs I can do?'

'You can sort the garage out if you want. Where's today's paper?'

He was trying to go into the kitchen again, but I needed to know if he was serious about the garage. 'I meant jobs for – you know – for money.'

'I don't mind paying up if the job's well done.'

'Can I help?' asked Jon, crashing down the bottom few stairs and landing in a heap at Dad's feet, like a naughty puppy. How dare he try to get in on my act, the wily little worm!

'Course you can,' said Dad, ruffling the worm's hair.

'That is so unfair, Dad! I'm the one who asked first. I really need that money badly.'

Dad interrupted his jovial mood to give me a frown – one of those narrow-eyed frowns that could go either way, and you just know you're treading a tightrope until you've got him safely back in Happyland. 'And to what can we attribute this sudden lack of funds?' he asked me, the frown deepening.

A wave of inspiration broke over me. 'I just seem to have far fewer clothes and things than all my friends.'

'Have you talked to your mum or Anne?'

The wave was a good one. It was still carrying me. 'I don't like to keep asking for stuff. That's why I want to earn some money.'

I could tell he approved of my answer. 'Fair enough. The garage it is then.'

'What about me?' said Jon, the loser.

'You can start doing jobs when you're a bit older, eh?'

And with that Dad went into the kitchen, and I avoided Jon's eyes as I legged it upstairs, leaving him sulking on the bottom stair.

3 MY MEGA SMART
BRAINWAVE

In my room I started thinking what I'd wear for my next trip to Ric's. I pulled one or two things out of my wardrobe and thought how babyish they looked compared with Claire's clothes. So I took a few more things out, and emptied all my drawers while I was at it, until in the end the whole bed and every bit of carpet were covered. Then I started picking through it all, arranging it into three piles – cool, uncool and too small. And as I did it, I thought fierce thoughts about Jon.

I'd lost count of the number of times I'd wanted to kill my stepbrother, but this time I reckoned he'd really got out of hand. I mean, it was definitely grounds for permanent separation. Actually, it wasn't the first time I'd considered separating from Jon. Nobody would mind if I wanted to live at Mum's instead of Dad's, but I know in my heart it's better for me to be here with Dad and Anne. I love Mum dearly, but we don't exactly – shall we say – see eye to eye. She and Dad are completely different from each other, and I've come out like Dad. We're more laid back, and we don't think about what we're going to do, we just do it.

It was when I was about five that Mum and Dad realised they weren't right for each other. Well, I expect they realised long before that, but they only decided to do something about it when I was five. I don't remember anything before then so I can't recall any rows or a bad atmosphere or anything. When they separated, Mum and I stayed in the house and Dad came round to visit us lots. We visited Dad in his new place too. Ever since they split my parents have always been totally friendly towards each other, and they still are now.

When I was about eight, Mum got a new partner, Colin. I didn't like having Colin around the place. It wasn't anything personal, just that I had less space. I also had less freedom because of there being two adults to dole out the rules, and that bugged me. Shortly after that, Dad met Anne. She and her son Jon moved in with Dad and, sucker that I am, I actually thought Jon was really sweet. I used to volunteer to play with him and look after him. I must have seemed like a too-good-to-be-true fairy to Anne. She really seemed to love me, and even though I was quite clumsy and kept breaking things, and I wasn't very bright at school, she forgave me everything because I was so devoted to little Jon. It was shortly after this that I asked Mum if I could go and live full-time at Dad's because I liked Jon so much. Mum and Colin were fine about it. Dad and Anne were delighted. So that's what happened.

Nowadays the four grown-ups all get on really well together. I once heard Claire's mum telling a friend of hers that my set-up was 'remarkably civilised'. I didn't know what she meant at the time, and when I asked Anne, she laughed and said Claire's mum meant it was good that everyone got on so well with each other.

When the three piles of clothes were complete, Anne looked at them in amazement.

'I can't believe it! I've never known you to be so organised. I'll take these two piles down to the Oxfam shop.' Then she caught sight of something which was practically brand new in the uncool pile. 'What are you getting rid of this for? I only bought it a few weeks ago.'

I look miles too young in it. Robby won't fancy me in that*!*

'It's a bit tight . . . under the arms . . .'

She nodded slowly. 'OK.'

After she'd gone out I looked through the clothes I was keeping. None of them were exactly stunning. I desperately needed some new stuff. Never mind, I'd be earning some money from clearing out the garage for Dad.

But then another thought hit me. I sat on the bed and flopped back. Clearing the garage out would pay off Snoopy downstairs, and might also stretch to some decent nail polish and lipstick. Big deal! To get all the things I wanted, I'd have to clear out garages every Saturday for the rest of the year.

And that's when my mega smart brainwave came out of the blue and hit me between the eyes. I would get a regular Saturday job. I was thirteen and I could make myself look fourteen. Surely I could wash up somewhere . . .

The brainwave shot up several planes.

I would get a job at the café where *he* worked – Ric's!

4 GOING FOR IT!

It was wet break at school the next day. Claire, Louisa, Kerry and I had managed to grab the warm corner and were sitting on the floor huddled round the heater. Claire was on her next-to-favourite subject (after the boy at the supermarket).

'Anyway, he comes over with the Coke and puts it down, and I'm like omigod! And Beth went *"Cheers, Robby"*, didn't you, Beth? And then – get this – he only smiled at her!'

Louisa and Kerry gasped and giggled. I loved

it that everyone was talking about him. I even made myself believe that he actually *had* smiled at me, and not just nodded.

'I can't wait to see him,' said Kerry.

'Me neither,' said Louisa.

I felt suddenly anxious, imagining what it would be like in the café – everyone watching me, knowing that I fancied Robby. 'He's very good looking and all that, but let's face it, he's not going to be interested in me, is he? He's about sixteen.'

Claire grabbed both my hands. 'Yeah, but wouldn't it be good if he was?' she squeaked.

Then it turned into a sort of group hug with all four of us giggling at the thought. But I couldn't giggle for long because I started imagining what it would be like if he walked in and saw us all like that. He'd think we were pathetic and girlie, and I didn't want to be like that. I wanted to be sensible and mature. And most of all I wanted to work at Ric's.

I'd spent ages lying in bed the night before, thinking about telling Claire that I was going to ask Mrs Tarr for a job. A little voice inside me had kept on at me that this was something I had to do on my own. It was important and it was serious. Claire and the others would find out, of course, but I didn't want everyone round me when I was talking to Mrs Tarr. I'd get embarrassed and tongue-tied, and then she'd think I was stupid, and even if there *was* a job going, she wouldn't want to offer it to a silly little girl like me. No, I'd wait till we'd all left Ric's, and had split up then I'd nip back a few minutes later.

As our group giggle broke up, a friend of Kerry's came along to show her something in a magazine, and the others all crowded round too. But I didn't. I went into a sort of daydream, staring at my friends and wondering how Robby would see them and how he'd see me.

Louisa's got pale skin and freckles. She's quite thin and always looks good, no matter what she's wearing – even school uniform. Her hair is fair too, and she doesn't have to think about it. It just hangs there, never greasy, in a bob. Kerry's dark with very short fashionable hair. She's obsessed with it – always washing it and fiddling with it in front of the mirror in the cloakroom. I've got long dark brown hair, a bit longer than shoulder length, and I'm about as thin as Kerry. Then there's Claire. We all know she's the best looking, with lovely creamy skin. But what else is it that makes her so wonderful? Is it her nose, her eyes, her mouth, her hair, her ears . . .?

And this was when I got my second big brainwave. Claire's got pierced ears. That's definitely part of her secret. There's nothing like earrings to make you look instantly older. For some unknown reason, Mum wasn't at all keen on 'young girls having their ears pierced', and she'd brainwashed Anne into having the same view. So the two of them had got together and come up with the magical age of fourteen for me to be allowed to have mine done. But I couldn't wait another three months. No way. I'd have to do a bit of heavy pleading. If I could convince Mum that it was a good thing, it would be no problem getting round Anne.

On the way to Ric's we called in at Claire's house. I tried on some of her things, but they didn't look right on me. I looked like a kid dressing up in its mum's clothes. I borrowed her make-up though and that made me look a bit more sophisticated. Then I brushed my hair till it shone.

As we walked into Ric's I got a huge attack of nerves, partly because of the thought of seeing Robby again and partly because of my plan to come back later and ask Mrs Tarr about a job.

In her short skirt and high wedges, Claire clicked purposefully over to the same table we'd had the previous day, sat down and picked up the menu. I followed her, wearing my most sensible expression, so that if Mrs Tarr was watching she might remember how mature I looked when I talked to her later. Kerry and Louisa, on the other hand, were staring round the whole café. Even when we'd sat down, and Claire was hissing at them to stop making it so obvious, they kept craning their necks trying to peer into every corner of the place.

'He's obviously in the kitchen!' hissed Claire.

But it was Mrs Tarr who came over to us, pad in hand. 'What are you having, girls?'

'Four Cokes,' said Claire.

I suddenly saw a chance to get Mrs Tarr to notice me. 'Actually, I'll have a lemonade, please,' I smiled at her.

Her mouth moved, but I can't exactly say it was a return smile. I bet she was a right battle-axe as an employer.

'Erm . . . is Robby here?' asked Claire.

'Afternoon off,' said Mrs Tarr.

My spirits sank to somewhere beneath the floorboards.

'Poor you,' said Claire, leaning forwards and giving a lovely sympathetic smile.

And in one way it *was* poor me, but in another way things couldn't have worked out better, because Claire decided it was a waste of time hanging round Ric's when she could be in the supermarket eyeing up the latest love of her life. So five minutes later she was gulping down her Coke, and the others were trying to keep up with her, but I was deliberately going slowly.

'I can't drink mine that quickly,' I said casually. 'And anyway I ought to get back home or Anne'll go spare. Give me your money and I'll pay when you've gone.'

'Oh come with us, Beth,' pleaded Claire. But it was only a half-hearted plea. She was flicking her hair about and thinking about Sunshine Supermarket Boy, I could tell.

'No, honestly, I've got to get back. Tell me what happened tomorrow, OK?'

And they went.

I slowly finished my drink while I kept an eye on Mrs Tarr, wondering when would be the best moment to approach her. I was also wondering what to say. I'd never asked anyone for a job before, and I didn't know whether there was a particular way of doing it.

As soon as I saw her at the till I went to pay. But it was just as though I was invisible. The moment she'd taken my money, she snapped the till shut and without looking to right or left, rushed off to the kitchen.

Great! Now I looked a complete idiot. I stood there for about two minutes, but everyone was in the kitchen. Then the youngest waitress emerged, tightly gripping a full tray and walking slowly and carefully. Maybe I should ask her about the job. So I followed right behind her, waited till she stopped, then said, 'Excuse me . . .'

Immediately she jumped about a mile in the air, the tray wobbled and a glass of lemonade tipped over and fell on the floor. The glass didn't break, but it rolled around and the lemonade went everywhere.

The waitress turned and looked daggers at me. 'What do you want?'

Everyone seemed to be staring at me, waiting to hear what I'd say.

I could hardly ask for a job now, so I just stood there, all red and embarrassed. She banged the tray down on the table, said, 'Back in a minute,' then rushed off to the kitchen.

This was a disaster. I should never have done it. If only I'd just gone with the others. Then someone tapped me on the shoulder and I turned round to see Mrs Tarr eyeing me with raised eyebrows.

I spoke in a whisper because the last thing I wanted was for anyone to hear what I was saying. 'I was wondering if you'd got any jobs washing up or anything?'

'Washing up?' boomed Mrs Tarr, in a voice loud enough for the whole street to hear. 'No, I'm not looking for anyone at present.'

'Oh . . . right . . .' Now what did I do? 'Erm . . . do you think you might be needing anyone some time soon?'

She sighed. 'No, I don't think I'll be needing anyone for the foreseeable future, but I'm afraid that even if I did need someone, they'd have to be considerably older than you.'

'I'm ... fourteen,' I told her. 'And I only meant Saturdays.'

'Fourteen! My goodness, I thought you were only twelve. Even so ...'

There were sniggers from a table nearby, which made me go red instantly, and suddenly I wanted to get out of the café. In fact I didn't know how I was ever going to dare show my face again. Twelve indeed! How dare she! The young waitress was giving me horrible looks as she wiped up the lemonade, and the other waitress was casting suspicious glances in my direction.

'Thanks anyway,' I mumbled. Then I shot out of the door as fast as I possibly could, feeling about six and a half.

5 AN EARLY BIRTHDAY PRESENT

When I got home, Anne was in the kitchen on the phone.

'Oh she's just walked in,' she said, raising her eyebrows at me, as if to ask me where I'd been. 'Hang on, I'll pass you over.' Then she whispered that it was Mum and handed me the phone.

'Sorry,' I said quietly to Anne. 'Madame Guernier was showing us something on the Internet.'

She nodded and I went through to the sitting room with the phone.

'Hiya, Mum.'

'Hello, darling.'

She sounded all bright and cheerful. I don't like it when people are in a good mood and I'm not. But hang on a sec . . . this would be the perfect chance to ask her about having my ears pierced. She was talking about something else now, but the moment I could get a word in edgeways, I'd go for it.

'The reason I phoned, Beth, was to see what we can do about getting you and Alisdair together.'

I had to crank my brain up a couple of gears to think who Alisdair was at first. Then I remembered – of course, they'd got Colin's son from Scotland staying with him. I've never met him, and it doesn't feel as though he's anything to do with me. I mean, I know he's my step-brother, but it's not the same as Jon. Jon lives with me. Jon's totally in my face the whole time, whereas Alisdair leads a completely separate life.

'His mum says it's amazingly difficult to get a job round where they live,' Mum was saying, 'and Alisdair asked if he could come and stay with us for a few weeks. He's already broken up because the Scottish school summer holidays are earlier than here. And quite honestly, he's a joy to have around.'

So Alisdair was going down well with my mum, was he? That meant he must be very bright, very neat and tidy, very *un*daring, and very very good. Yuk! I hated him before I'd even set eyes on him.

'He's such a lovely boy, Bethany. You must meet him.' *No, I mustn't.* 'He's managed to get a job at Townley's. You know, they're a firm of independent financial advisors. Isn't that brilliant? He's answering the phone and filling in forms and everything.'

'Yeah, brilliant.' I had to admit it, I was slightly impressed. I was thinking of the Year Eleven boys at school. I couldn't imagine any of them managing to get a job at a place like Townley's. But then they weren't geeks, were they?

'I'm not really surprised, you know. His employers can obviously see that he's a very bright boy. He's been predicted ten A stars at GCSE, you know!' All I knew was that Mum would be smiling her head off at the other end of the phone. It made me sick. Why were adults so impressed with brightness? Why should that be their Number One thing? 'Why don't you pop over on Saturday and meet him?'

Saturday? No chance!

'The trouble is, I promised Dad I'd clear out the garage for him, and it'll take most of the day.'

'Oh dear, and Sunday we're off to the Hamiltons in Norfolk for the day.'

'Never mind, Mum,' I said in a nice bright voice. 'There's always the next weekend.'

'Yes, that's true.'

And now for the six-million-dollar question. 'Mum . . .'

'Mm?'

'I was wondering if I could ask you a big favour . . .'

'Mmmm?'

'The thing is, I'm the only one in the class who hasn't got their ears pierced and I feel really babyish . . .'

'Well, you won't feel babyish in three months' time, will you?'

'Oh no! I can't wait that long!'

'Sorry, love. I'm not changing my mind.'

I could tell from her voice that there was no point in arguing. She was sticking with her decision. I could hardly be bothered to talk to her after that. So while she rambled on about the wonderful Alisdair, I started hatching a rather scary plan.

There was no way Anne was going to agree to letting me have my ears pierced when Mum was so dead against it, but what if I pretended that Mum had changed her mind? Mum would never find out from Anne. She and Anne only really talked on the phone when Mum rang up to speak to me, so as long as I made sure I did lots of phoning, then Mum would never need to phone here, would she? And I could borrow some clip-on earrings from Claire's old dressing-up box to cover up the holes in my ears whenever I was seeing Mum! Brilliant! Sorted.

As soon as Mum and I had rung off, I went into the kitchen. Anne was dashing around getting ingredients out for an instant meal.

'Guess what!' I began. 'Mum doesn't mind about me having my ears pierced.'

'Oh!'

'So *can* I?'

She pulled a drawer out of the freezer, rummaged through the contents, pushed it back in again and pulled out another one. 'Are you sure?'

'Yeah, she really doesn't mind at all. She's totally cool about it!'

'Well, if you're sure . . .'

The secret is to get them when they're concentrating on something else. This was going so well.

'Could I have an advance on my allowance? Just this once.'

I hoped I hadn't overdone it. That last bit was probably pushing my luck. She stopped rummaging and frowned. I couldn't tell if she was frowning at whatever was in that particular freezer drawer, or because of what I'd just said. She looked at me. The frown was still there. It was a big one. Uh-oh!

'I don't know anything about ear-piercing these days. How much is it? Do you need an appointment or what?'

This was turning out to be such a doddle. Why hadn't I thought of doing it before?

'Claire made an appointment at that new place on Welby Street. It cost her seventeen pounds fifty.'

'Seventeen pounds fifty! That's a lot of money. If I start advancing you big sums like that, you'll forever be behind . . .'

I'd been feeling so hopeful and now all that hope was going down the drain. One last try . . .

'I'll do jobs every weekend until I've paid it off.'

'Hmm. Didn't your mum offer to pay?'

I gulped and shook my head.

'Hmmmmm. I'll talk to your dad about it.'

OK. Only don't talk to Mum about it, or I'll be on Mars with no return ticket.

* * *

That evening I cleared up after the meal, loaded the dishwasher, helped Jon with his poem for school the next day, made coffee for Anne and Dad, washed up the pans and things that were in the sink, wiped the surfaces until they gleamed, swept the floor and gave Dad loads of hugs and kisses.

You see, Anne had obviously had a word with my lovely dad when he'd come back from work, and over the meal, they'd told me that they'd decided to pay for me to have my ears pierced. Anne was going to make the appointment and I could regard it as part of my birthday present – the early part. Brilliant! I might not have got a job at Ric's, but at least I was on the way to making Robby notice me. And that was the most important thing of all.

6 COOL IMAGE – HUH!

I looked at my watch for the tenth time. Nine forty-two. Why was Saturday morning passing at such a mind-numbingly slow speed? I'd spent forty-two minutes on this garage and it didn't look much different from how it had looked in the first place. It was only the thought of the five pounds at the end of it that was keeping me going. I'd got my radio on in the corner and every time they played a good song I managed to work a bit faster. It kind of pushed my spirits up and made me think of what a great afternoon I was going to have.

At two-thirty I'd be so scared I'd probably faint (except that Claire would be there to hold my hand), and less than five minutes later I'd be in heaven, on my way to Ric's with little gold studs in my ears. I'd be wearing my very coolest clothes, which still weren't anything like as cool as Claire's – but who cares? I'd managed to borrow a fantastic belt from her which was blue, purple, pink and silver. I'd also managed to get my hair up into a messy bun, which I'd been trying to do for the last year, but my hair had never been long enough till this very morning. I planned to use some of Anne's make-up, and with the earrings, I knew I was going to feel a whole lot better than the last time I was in the café.

As I sorted out every single nail and screw and bit of rusty metal that had been dumped in one of the drawers of this enormous chest on the back wall of the garage, I started day-dreaming.

I was right in the middle of getting married to Robby, wearing a slinky white dress, with Claire trailing after me in a yukky pink fluffy job, when Anne came charging into the garage and asked me if I minded looking after Jon and Alex for the afternoon.

'But you said I was allowed to go with Claire to have my ears pierced. I don't want Jon and Alex there too, do I?'

'Don't worry about that. Your dad'll look after the boys while I'm with you and Claire in the beautician's. Then Dad and I can get straight off to the garden centre afterwards and you can look after the boys till we're back. We'll be as quick as we can.'

Uh-oh! This was getting desperate. The last thing I wanted was Jon and Alex hanging around while I was trying to impress Robby.

'But I want to go on to Ric's with Claire and the others.'

'I thought you were short of money?'

'I am but my friends are all going, so I want to. Anyway, I'm earning money at the moment, aren't I?'

'Hm.'

'Oh please don't make me take them, Anne. They'll ruin it.'

And then she just looked at me. And we both knew what the look meant. *Don't you think it's the least you can do to take your little brother and his friend into town when Dad and I have paid for you to have your ears pierced?*

I sighed a big sigh and went back to the nails and screws. 'OK.' And then I thought, in for a penny, in for a pound. 'They may as well tag along while I'm having my ears pierced.'

'Good girl.'

And when I next looked up, she'd gone out.

The rest of the morning went more slowly than ever. Even the good songs on the radio didn't help it go faster. By twelve o'clock I'd really had enough.

'Stupid pathetic thing!' I snarled at the drawer I was trying to put back in. It was completely jammed, not letting me pull it out again *or* push it in.

In the end I yanked it with all my might and it came shooting out. Unfortunately it made me topple backwards, and I trod awkwardly on the pile of things I'd got ready to chuck out. I felt a sharp little stab of pain in my ankle before I lost my balance and fell on my bottom. My hand landed on an old door hinge in the rubbish pile, and although I didn't actually draw blood, it hurt.

I was furious by then, and started struggling up before anyone came in and saw me in that state. But it was agony trying to put my weight on my right foot, and I flopped straight back on to my bottom again.

Oh great! I'm going to look stunning, aren't I, in my cool clothes with my snazzy belt, lovely studs, trendy hair and a limp!

Jon giggled at me all the way down to Welby Street because I was limping. Claire kept telling me to ignore him, but it was all right for her – she was wearing an even higher than normal pair of wedges that she'd borrowed from her sister. I had been going to wear her old ones, but my foot hurt too much when I tried them on, so I was limping along in my trainers. The other thing that was hacking me off was my hair. The bun had looked really good in my bedroom, but from the moment I'd started hobbling along, bits of it had fallen down, so by the time we were at the beautician's I must have looked as though I'd been in an argument with a load of brambles.

'Shall I take this scrunchie out?' I asked Claire.

She hesitated. That meant yes.

'No, it looks really good,' said Alex, going deep pink (so attractive in a nine-year-old!).

'I'm definitely taking it out then,' I said just loudly enough for Alex to hear. Then I yanked it off a bit harder than I'd meant to, forgetting that there were several grips in my hair. 'I've come to have my ears pierced,' I smiled at the receptionist.

'Name?'

'Bethany Austin.'

'Brought your fan club?' she asked me, nodding at Claire and the others. I laughed for about one second then realised she wasn't amused. She gave another nod in the general direction of a few chairs, and said, 'They'll have to wait there.' Then she buzzed through to somewhere or other: 'I've got Bethany Austin in reception.'

A moment later a girl in a white coat came to get me.

'Good luck!' said Claire and the others as I was led away. The last voice I heard was Alex's, 'Good luck, Bethany. Hope it doesn't hurt too much.'

'It won't hurt at all,' the girl in the white coat informed me. In the little mirrored room, she sat me down and asked me if I wanted the larger or the smaller studs. I chose the larger, of course. Then she drew a pair of black dots on my ears and told me to look at them through the mirror and tell her if I thought they were in the right place. That made me nervous. I mean, you would have thought she would have known where to put the dots without having to ask me, wouldn't you?

'I *think* it's OK,' I said, giving her an anxious look.

She didn't say anything to that, just came at

me with a gun which stank of disinfectant, and bang!

'That's one done.'

I couldn't believe it. I hadn't felt a thing. Not a single thing. She did the other one just as fast and gave me the mirror to look in. I couldn't stop grinning and turning my head from side to side to admire each ear separately. It was amazing that they could shoot the studs in just like that! I absolutely loved them.

When I went back to the others, they loved them too, especially Alex. The moment we were out of the building, he wanted to touch them.

'No,' I snapped. 'I don't want them to get infected.'

'Aaah,' gooed Claire. 'Don't be horrible to him.'

'She isn't!' Alex told Claire quite aggressively, which made her fall about laughing.

'Come on, let's go to Ric's!' I said, feeling suddenly very excited.

'My mum's given me some money for the café,' said my number one fan.

'Couldn't they go and spend their pocket money while we're at Ric's, then come and meet us afterwards?' Claire suggested.

'Anne said I mustn't let them out of my sight.'

Claire put her arm round me and whispered that we'd stick them on another table as far away as possible from us, so I could concentrate on looking sexy for Robby. A big surge of nerves came over me when she said his name.

When we got to Ric's, Claire went in first and I was last. Robby was at the till, looking gorgeous. He happened to look up just at the right moment because Claire was marching Jon and Alex off to a table for two at the opposite side of the café from where Louisa and Kerry had got a table for four. I gave him a shaky smile then felt my heart lurching all over the place because he smiled back at me. And this time there was no question about it.

Please don't let Mrs Tarr say anything about me asking for a job, I said over and over when I spotted her eyeing me from the counter. But then my mind was totally taken up with Robby because he was standing there, pad in hand, pen poised.

But unfortunately Jon had come over at the same time. I could have killed him. 'Can you order for us too?' he asked me.

'Yes, OK,' I said, trying not to sound snappy and shaking my head to make sure my hair wasn't covering my lovely new studs.

'Pooh, that stuff on your ears really stinks!' said Jon.

7 THE UPS AND THE BIG DOWNER

'Sit like this, Beth,' said Claire, arranging herself with one of her shoulders sticking out and her head tipped to the side.

I tried it, but I just felt stupid. Robby was taking absolutely no notice of me anyway. He was just getting on with his job, quietly and thoroughly. Every so often Mrs Tarr smiled at him. It was obvious she thought he was the best thing since the mobile phone. The young waitress from the other day wasn't there, thank goodness – just the one who'd looked at me suspiciously.

She must have still been giving me suspicious looks because Louisa suddenly piped up, 'Do you know that waitress or something?'

'Only about as well as I know Mary Magdalene,' I replied loudly, on the off chance that Robby might hear and think I was really witty.

'Mary who?' asked Kerry.

Louisa was looking at me blankly too, so then I felt even more stupid.

'I'm just going to the loo,' Claire suddenly said. Then she leaned over and whispered, 'Watch me!' with a twinkle in her eye.

She'd timed it so that she'd be walking right in front of Robby and he'd have to stop to let her go through. She was wiggling her hips like mad. It was a bit over the top, but it might be worth trying. After all, nothing else had worked.

'Uh-oh,' said Kerry. 'Something tells me Jon wants to get going, Beth.'

I looked over to see Jon sitting sideways in his chair, so he was facing us, with his arms folded and a big scowl on his face.

'I'd better have a word,' I sighed, as I got up and headed off, trying for a subtle touch of hip swing but not a big obvious wiggle.

Unfortunately I'd completely forgotten about my ankle, and after two steps I had to stop and grab hold of the back of a chair, gasping and doubled over in pain.

'Are you all right?'

It was him. The idol. The chosen one. His hand was on my back. I nearly fainted – and not with pain.

'Yeah. Sorry. I twisted my ankle earlier, and I got up too quickly just then.'

'Sure you're OK?'

I nodded and put on my bravest face to go limping off. What a result! I couldn't resist turning round to see if the others had been watching. They had. They were both thumbing up like mad. I must have been grinning my head off by the time I got to Jon's table.

'We're bored,' said Jon. 'When are we going? We've been here ages.'

'We won't be long.' I caught sight of Robby taking someone's money at the counter. *Yes, we will.*

'It's OK,' said Alex, the devoted one. 'We don't mind staying here, do we, Jon?'

'Yes we do,' said Jon. 'At least *I* do. Can't we just go and spend our pocket money?'

I thought about what Anne had said. 'I'm not supposed to let you out of my sight.'

'Oh, go on . . . We'll come straight back.'

I frowned. Maybe it would be all right.

'Go on . . .' he pleaded.

'Well, as long as you don't cross any roads and you come back here in ten minutes.'

'Ten minutes? That's nothing.'

'No, mate, *nothing* is what it'll be if you argue,' I told him.

I couldn't help glancing round to see if Robby had heard that one. But he must have gone through to the kitchen.

'You fancy that waiter, don't you?' grinned Jon.

I practically bit his head off. 'Course I don't!'

'Here's the money that Mum gave me when I told her we'd be coming here,' said Alex, trying to change the subject. He must have been clutching the coins for ages. They were really hot.

I got back to our table at the same time as Claire.

'Guess what!' said Kerry. 'Robby stopped and asked Beth if she was all right, because of her ankle hurting. He even put his hand on her back.'

Claire gave me a big hug, then kissed me on

both cheeks like the French do. 'He so fancies you, Beth!' she squealed.

'Ssh!' I said, excitement buzzing and gurgling about inside me.

'I wish *my* ankle was sprained!' giggled Kerry.

And we were all laughing away when Mrs Tarr suddenly appeared. Something tightened inside me as she started talking to me as though we'd known each other for years.

'It looks as though there might be a job coming up after all – a waitressing job.'

'Oh! Right,' I stammered, feeling myself going pink.

'It's not absolutely definite but it's a possibility. I need an extra pair of hands on Saturdays from twelve till five. That's our really busy time.' She gave me a searching look then asked, 'Are you a hard worker?'

'Very!' I said with a shaky smile.

I could feel the others' eyes on me, and I was

getting quite nervous about what they were going to say afterwards. But there was another feeling, much bigger than the nervousness, that was bubbling up inside me. It was a brilliant excitement. I was going to have a job – a real proper grown-up job. With him!

'I can be more definite in a few days, but in the mean time, why don't you write your details down for me – name, address, phone number?'

'OK.' She was moving away. 'Th-thank you!' I called after her.

She turned round and gave me a little nod and a smile. Then there was a silence at our table. I looked at the others. They were staring at me, mouths open.

Claire broke the silence first. She did one of those ecstatic screams and grabbed my hand.

'Bethy, why didn't you tell us? How did you think of it? You're so clever!'

I could have hugged her. I could have hugged

everyone in the café. 'The idea just popped into my head when you'd all left the café the other day, so I decided to go for it.'

'You kept it jolly quiet,' grinned Louisa.

'I forgot about it, because Mrs Tarr said there wasn't anything going.'

'Hey! Where are Jon and Alex?' said Kerry.

'It's OK. They've gone to spend their pocket money. They'll be back in a minute,' I said.

So we talked about my job and how lucky I was, working with someone I fancy.

Then Louisa suddenly said, 'They've been gone a long time.'

I looked at my watch and gasped.

'Let's go and look for them,' said Claire. 'It should be easy with four of us.'

But at that very moment, Alex came rushing into the café.

'Bethany,' he called out as he belted over to our table with a very white face.

'What's the matter?' I asked him, gripping his shoulders to make him tell me more quickly.

'Jon's broken something in a gift shop,' he said shakily. 'The man's really cross about it. Jon's got to pay for it. I came to find you, because we didn't know what to do.'

I felt sick. This was the very worst thing that could have happened. 'What shop?'

'Kellet's.'

'Omigod!'

Kellet's is a very popular gift shop with all sorts of fantastic things in it – some of them really expensive. 'What did he break?' I managed to ask, gulping.

'A big vase.'

'Oh no! Anne'll kill me for letting him out of my sight!'

'There's glass everywhere.'

Great!

8 MY IMPRESSIVE
STEPBROTHER – YUK!

Claire walked home with me and Jon and Alex,
which was nice of her. The other two had gone
to Kerry's. Who could blame them for not
wanting to stick around with a load of misery
guts like us. Jon was biting his hand, which was
a thing he used to do when he was little and was
worried about something.

'So why *did* you give the man your mum's
number instead of Anne's?' asked Claire. 'I don't
get you.'

'Because Anne'd go spare. She's only just

forked out for these earrings, hasn't she? *And* I didn't do what she asked me to do – I let Jon out of my sight.'

Jon stopped biting his hand for long enough to speak. 'But what if the man in the shop tells your mum the truth and says it was a boy who broke the vase? Then she'll be sure to tell Mum, and Mum'll kill me.'

'Stop worrying about it, Jon. *I'm* the only one who's got to worry.' I was trying to sound big-sisterly and firm, because I really did feel sorry for him, he seemed so scared.

'Yeah, *you'll* be all right, Jon,' said Claire kindly. 'You heard what the shopkeeper said when Beth told him to say it was her fault because she was supposed to be looking after you. He just said, "I don't care whose name I write down, as long as I get it paid for." '

Jon was biting his hand so hard I thought he was going to bite it off. 'Yeah, but . . .'

And suddenly I realised why he was quaking in his shoes. He wasn't worried about Anne. He was worried that Anne might tell his dad. Because he knew that if his dad got to hear about it, he'd be in deep trouble. His dad's quite scary. I mean, *I* think he's scary, and he's not even my dad. Jon doesn't see him very often at all. In fact *my* dad's more like a real dad to him. Poor old Jon!

'Maybe your mum's out, Beth,' said Claire. 'Just think, if she doesn't get in till after five-thirty, the man won't be able to phone her till Monday morning. Who knows, perhaps he might have cooled down by then and decided to forget all about it.'

For the first time, I felt a tiny ray of hope.

'Yeah,' I said, slowly, turning towards her. 'That'd be good.'

But no sooner had she given me the hope than she whipped it away again. 'Let's hope your mum doesn't find out about the earrings at the same time as the vase. Wow! Just think how furious she'd be if *that* happened!'

I stopped in my tracks and gasped. I'd completely forgotten about the earrings. Oh, what a complete and utter mess!

As soon as we got home I tried to phone Mum, because I wanted to talk to her before she talked to Anne. But it was the answerphone. Good.

I tried every five minutes till five-thirty when Anne and Dad got home. Answerphone every time. Good. Now there was a chance that I might be let off till Monday. And as Claire said, that might mean that I'd be let off altogether.

Anne and Dad were in a brilliant mood because they'd found two garden loungers that were half price. Their bargain buys made them think the whole world was wonderful.

'Nice ears!' said Dad, grinning at me and having a closer look.

'Did she tell you to twist them round night and morning?' asked Anne, also smiling away.

I nodded and tried to look happy, but it wasn't easy.

'Is that ankle still hurting, love?'

'Yeah, a bit' (which wasn't a complete lie).

'And what about you?' asked Dad, turning to Jon. 'What did you spend your pocket money on, young man?'

John went pale and gulped. I didn't even know if he'd spent his pocket money. We'd never discussed it with all the vase drama.

'He bought loads of sweets and ate most of them,' I said, on a sudden burst of inspiration.

'Tut tut! Teeth!' said Anne. 'Never mind, I'll let you off this once – you're not usually bad.'

Then the phone ran and I lurched across the room, trying to grab it before anyone else did.

'Hello, love,' came Mum's bright voice. I whispered to Anne and Dad that it was for me, then shot out of the kitchen, heart banging. 'What have you been up to?'

My antennae were out, trying to detect the teensiest hint of crossness. So far, so good.

'I'm fine. I tried to phone you a bit earlier . . .'

'We've only just got in, love. Is everything OK?'

I felt as though I'd just survived Round One of a world title boxing match. 'Yes, everything's fine. I just phoned for a chat.'

'So what have you been up to?'

Having my ears pierced? Nope. Fancying waiters? Nope. Not looking after my stepbrother properly? Nope. Deceiving my stepmother? Nope. Getting a job? Maybe that would be a good one? Would she approve? Better not risk it.

'Nothing much.' This was ridiculous. She must have wondered why ever I'd rung up in the first place if I didn't have anything to say. I searched around in my poor tired brain. 'Er . . . how's Colin?'

'Colin?' Mum sounded as though I'd just asked after one of her long-dead ancestors or something. I suppose it wasn't the kind of thing I usually asked.

'He's . . . fine.' Her voice went into liquid cherry mode. 'And so is Alisdair.' Oh yeah, Alisdair. I'd forgotten about him but Mum hadn't. I could feel her glowing and beaming at the other end of the phone. 'It sounds as though he's doing terribly well at Townley's. He works so hard we hardly ever see him, because when he's not at work he's off exploring.'

'Exploring?'

'I know,' she laughed. 'I said to Colin, "Fancy a boy of that age wanting to go off on his own!" He takes his camera with him with him, you know, but he's never shown us any photos. He says we wouldn't be interested. And to tell you the truth, I don't think we would.'

'Why not?'

'Well, he says all his pictures are things like close-ups of a particular tree, or a lamppost or something like that.' I wasn't surprised Mum wasn't very impressed. She preferred photos of good views and old churches and boring things like that. 'He's gone off with his camera again today – I don't know where. But he said he'd be back about five or six, so I expect he'll be walking in at any minute.'

Good. The sooner the better, because then she couldn't talk about him any more. I'd had a gut full of Alisdair talk. 'OK, then.'

But Mum obviously wanted to make quite sure I was left in no doubt at all about exactly how impressive my stepbrother was. 'I must say, when he *is* here, he's a joy to have around. I honestly didn't know boys could be so neat and tidy. He even cleans the bath out every time he uses it. What do you think about that!'

I think . . . I feel sick.

9 PARENTS – YOU NEVER CAN TELL!

Mondays are generally the pits – double science, double geography, double history and French. But this Monday was ten times worse than usual.

Before breakfast Jon had come bursting into my room.

'The man in the shop'll definitely phone your mum today, and he's sure to say it was me what did it, and then your mum'll phone mine and –'

'Calm down!' I told him, even though I was a nervous wreck myself.

At breakfast time, he was all white, and kept on stuffing his fist in his mouth.

'Toast not done to your satisfaction today, Jon?' joked Dad. 'Prefer to eat your fist, do you?'

'What's the matter, Jon?' Anne asked. 'You've got a face as long as the Nile.'

I gave Jon a piercing glare to send him the clear message that 'Nothing' would be a good reply.

'Nothing.'

Good. He got the message.

But Jon couldn't help his emotions showing, and a few minutes later Anne tried again.

'Just tell us what's the matter,' she said in a kindly tone. 'We won't be cross.'

And then Jon made the stupid mistake of saying, 'You *will*.'

The glare I gave him this time would have wiped out whole nations if it had been a nuclear glare.

'No, we won't,' Dad added in a firm voice. 'Come on, what is it?'

'Nothing,' said Jon, seeing me urgently mouthing '*Chill!*'

Anne and Dad exchanged a suspicious look, and I knew I'd have to give Jon a lecture after breakfast, because I could bet anything that Anne would wait till she was driving him to school, then tackle him when they were alone in the car.

'If she asks you again, say you're worried because you've got a test at school, OK?' I hissed at him on the landing.

He nodded, but I wasn't convinced he'd taken it in.

At morning break I got talking with Claire and the others. They were all being ultra kind and sympathetic, and telling me everything would be fine, which is easy to say when you're not actually stuck in the middle of the nightmare yourself.

'It's good that your mum was out till after five-thirty, anyway,' said Louisa.

'Yeah,' said Kerry. 'Let's just hope that the bloke from the shop doesn't tell her that it was a boy who actually broke the vase.'

'But I told him not to,' I squealed, feeling a big spurt of panic coming on.

'Yeah, but all the same . . .'

Oh great!

'Are you coming down to Ric's after school?' asked Claire, obviously going for a subtle change of conversation to cheer me up.

'I think I'd better go home to face the music.'

'But Mrs Tarr might have some news about the job,' said Kerry.

I sighed. 'I wouldn't dare take it even if she did,' I said. 'It'd be just another thing to add to my criminal record.'

'Er . . . do you mind if *I* go for it, then?' asked Claire, looking a bit embarrassed.

I shook my head, and thought how unfair life was. I'd be at home getting an earful from Mum on the phone while Claire would be landing herself a job at the café, thanks to me.

Anne was in the kitchen when I got back from school.

'Hi. Had a good day?'

'Boring science, even more boring geography, excruciatingly boring history and not-too-bad French.'

'Oh well, at least French saved the day.'

'And I hope you're pleased that I came straight home. Claire and the others went down to Ric's.'

'Yes, I am.' She rewarded me with a smile. 'I'm surprised the others can afford to keep going there.'

'Claire's going to try and get a job there – a Saturday job.'

'Oh, that's a good idea.'

What? Did I need a hearing test?

'You think it's a good idea to have a job in the café?'

'Yes, I do. So long as you don't get too tired and you still have time to do your homework, I'm all in favour of working to earn a bit of money, and I think a café job's much safer than, say, doing a paper round.'

'But I could have got the job myself! I only didn't because I thought you wouldn't approve!'

'No, not at all. Is it too late to say you want it? I can run you down there if you like.'

I didn't really want Anne coming into the café when all my friends were around. 'It's OK, I'll walk. See you later.'

'Take care, now!'

* * *

'Has Mrs Tarr said anything about the job?' I puffed as I catapulted through the door and landed in a heap at Claire's table. It looked like she and the others were just leaving.

'Yes, I'm doing it!' beamed Claire. 'Starting on Saturday. Isn't it great?'

'Great,' I said flatly as I flopped into the spare chair.

'You don't exactly seem on cloud nine about it,' commented Kerry.

'What are you doing here, anyway?' asked Louisa.

'I told Anne that Claire was going for a job here, and she totally shocked me by saying it was a pity I didn't do that myself!'

Claire looked alarmed.

'Oh no!' said Kerry. 'Now it seems *really* unfair that you've got it, Claire. I mean Beth asked first, didn't she?'

I suddenly remembered Robby then. 'Is he here?' I whispered to the others.

They didn't need to ask who I meant. Louisa nodded at the counter and I turned round to have a look. He saw me looking and gave me a sort of shy smile.

'Did you see that? He just smiled at you,' whispered Kerry, who was facing the till.

Claire turned round extremely unsubtly then whipped straight back. 'He's gone red. That proves it. He definitely must fancy you, Bethy. You'll *have* to work here. I can't take the job. It's just not fair.'

I could have hugged her.

'But if *I* take it, *I'll* feel unfair now.'

'Not as unfair as me.'

'Ask!' hissed Louisa.

Mrs Tarr was just walking past our table. 'Excuse me . . .'

She pulled out a pad and I launched straight

in before I could change my mind.

'You know the job? Well, it turns out that I *can* do it after all, and Claire says she doesn't mind, so I just wanted to check if that's OK . . .'

'I don't mind which one of you does it, as long as I don't get any problems. You'd be on trial for the first couple of Saturdays to check you're up to it, anyway.'

I nodded enthusiastically.

'I'll provide you with an apron, but I want you to be dressed cleanly and smartly and with your hair tied back at all times. Twelve o'clock till five, as I said, and you can start next week. You'll need to be here a few minutes early.'

I nodded hard and thanked her over and over again. Then when she'd gone, the others let out great squeals of delight, while I tried to shush them because I had to prove that I was well past the squealing age. I was, in fact, about to become a member of the adult world of work. And what was more, I would be working with *him*. And this time, it wasn't just a castle in the air. It was for real.

10 LEARNING THE ROPES

At ten to twelve on Saturday morning I went into the café, feeling nervous and excited.

'Well done. Nice and punctual,' said Mrs Tarr, striding out of nowhere and trying to smile, but not really managing it. 'Let's throw you in at the deep end. Come through to the kitchen.' I followed meekly. I thought I was going to feel so grown up, and yet I felt really babyish. 'This is Adrian, the chef . . .'

I smiled. Adrian nodded at me through the steam. He was tall and red faced, but I couldn't tell if that was because it was so hot in the kitchen. 'And you're . . .?'

'Bethany.'

'Nice one, Bethany.'

Then he went back to his pans.

'This is Robby . . .'

I'd forgotten about him because of feeling so nervous about everything else, but now he was standing right in front of me, I felt my stomach wobble about. 'Hello, Robby.'

I liked saying his name.

'This is Bethany, Robby. She's our new Saturday waitress.'

'Tell me if you need any help with anything,' he said in a soft voice. I noticed that he'd got a pink bit at the tops of his cheeks.

'OK,' I said.

'I'll be back in a minute,' said Mrs Tarr. And she went rushing through to the café, leaving me standing there like a spare part.

'Show Bethany the ropes, then,' Adrian called over his shoulder, because Robby was hopping from foot to foot, looking even more spare than I felt.

'Oh yeah. Right . . . Well, Adrian rings a little bell when he's got an order ready for you to take. Any of us can take food to any table. You just ask Adrian what table it's for, then you take it.'

'Here you go. That lot's for number seven,' called Adrian. He had to speak loudly because of all the noise from the air extractors and the oven fans and a machine that was whirring and clonking.

'That's the dishwasher,' said Robby, seeing me looking. 'You probably won't have to know how to work it. I'll . . . er . . . just take these through,' he went on, still looking pink. 'Back in a minute.'

My body tingled. I still couldn't believe I was

actually here, working with him. And he seemed to genuinely like me. I pinched myself to check it really *was* happening.

'Take a butcher's in there,' Adrian told me, nodding in the direction of a separate little room attached to the kitchen. The door was open so I went to look. This was the washing-up area. There were two huge sinks with very long draining boards. 'You'll have to wash the odd pan and any stuff that I need in a hurry, or if we've got so much in the dishwasher that there's no room left.'

I felt as though I should be making some kind of witty reply, but I couldn't think of anything to say, so I stayed quiet. Then Mrs Tarr came back.

'Good, you're having a look round. Let me get you an apron then we'll pop through and I'll explain how the tables are numbered and show you how to take an order. Now, the big thing is not to panic. Just stay calm, write clearly so Adrian can read it, be polite to the customers, and if they ask you anything that you can't answer, you simply say, "I'm sorry, I'm very new here. I'll just go and ask." Oh, and call me Sue, by the way. All right?'

It seemed like Mrs Tarr (I'd never get used to calling her Sue) wasn't such a battle-axe after all.

Ten minutes later, I felt as though I was at least two years older. It was such a cool feeling, the first time I wrote down an order. I had to give Adrian the top paper, and stick the duplicate on this board behind the counter. The numbers one to ten, representing the tables, were written on the board, and each number had a hook sticking out of it. So when you jabbed the paper on the hook you knew which table had had what, when it came to making up the bill at the end.

I couldn't wait to tell Claire and the others about it. I'd told them they weren't allowed to come in today, on pain of death, because I knew how nervous I was going to be and I thought I'd be even worse if they were all watching me. But I really wished they could see me at work now I was feeling more confident.

'Are you working here for the whole summer?' I asked Robby when we were both in the kitchen. It had taken me ages to pluck up the courage to ask him.

'Maybe,' he answered. Then he turned away, as though he didn't want to talk.

I wished I hadn't asked. I didn't want him to think I was being nosy.

'Number two's order is ready,' called Adrian. 'And number three's is just coming. Could you wash some pans and things for me, Bethany?'

So Robby picked up number two's order and I went through to the little washing-up room.

A few minutes later Robby came up behind me. He spoke in his usual soft voice. 'Your friends are in there. The one called Claire asked me to tell you.'

He was a bit red again, and I wondered whether he was just very shy around girls.

So they'd come after all, had they? I finished the washing-up as fast as I could because I was dying to see them. When I went through I gave them a little wave then went straight over to clear a table because some customers were just leaving. I took the dirty dishes through then came back with a cloth and wiped the table thoroughly.

'You're doing well,' said Mrs Tarr – Sue – giving me a nice smile.

When I'd laid the table up, I nipped over to see Claire and the others.

'You're really good at it, Beth,' said Claire, grabbing my hand. 'I mean you look like a proper waitress.'

'She *is* a proper waitress,' said Kerry.

'You don't mind us being here, do you?' asked Louisa anxiously.

I shook my head. 'I'm used to it now, so I'm not nervous any more.'

'What's it like working with Robby?' whispered Claire, leaning forwards, eyes gleaming.

'It's good,' was all I could think of saying. 'He's really nice.'

'He took our order,' said Claire, 'and he went all pink when I asked him to tell you that we were here.'

'I think he's quite shy,' I said.

'But does he talk to you much now you're working with him?'

I thought about Robby's one-word answer when I'd asked him about the job. Claire was wrinkling her nose as though she was expecting me to say, 'No, he seems a real drag,' but I didn't, because I felt like defending him, for some unknown reason.

'We don't really get the chance to talk,' I said.

'I'm going to ask him some questions when he next comes over to our table,' said Claire, with a gleam in her eye.

And I wasn't sure why I felt like this, but I really didn't want her to do that.

'Guess where we're going after this?' she then asked, changing the subject.

'I don't suppose you'd be on your way to see Checkout Charlie, by any chance?' I asked, jokingly.

'I'm determined to find out his name today,' grinned Claire. 'Then you won't be able to take the rip out of me any more.'

I saw Mrs Tarr looking in my direction, and suddenly realised I shouldn't be standing about chatting with my friends like this.

'I'd better go.'

'Give us a ring later,' called Claire.

All the way home from the café, I clutched my wages inside my pocket as I thought about everything that had happened. I felt pleased because I'd survived the afternoon without anything terrible happening. Mrs Tarr – Sue – had patted me on the back and said, 'Well done.' Robby had still been there when I'd finished, and it was lovely saying, 'See you next week,' as I went off.

'Yeah, seeya,' he'd said in his soft voice. Then he'd added, 'Take care,' and my stomach had wobbled about again, which really got me confused. I thought I didn't fancy him any more, but now I wasn't sure again.

As soon as I'd told Anne and Dad all about my afternoon, I phoned Claire. I was expecting her to ask me about work, because she and the others had gone almost directly after our chat.

But she didn't. Instead she started telling me about how they'd gone to the supermarket, and they'd got as far as the car park and *the* boy was just coming out of the supermarket. Apparently Claire had plucked up all her courage and gone racing over and started asking him whether the supermarket was open the next day or not. He'd said he didn't know and he didn't care, and then he'd asked her what she was called and she'd told him. Then she'd found out that he was called Guy, and then – 'Get this, Beth, he actually offered to walk me home!'

Claire was really screeching down the phone with excitement when she told me this bit. I had to admit I was a bit jealous – not because Robby hadn't offered to walk me home, but because I suddenly realised I couldn't possibly fancy Robby. I wasn't bursting to talk about him like Claire was, and I didn't have that same buzzy feeling any more.

Once Claire had finished telling me every single detail of how Guy didn't walk her home in the end, because his mates turned up and started jeering at him for talking to a girl, she finally asked me how the rest of my afternoon had gone.

'I like the job,' I told her. 'But I've realised I don't fancy Robby . . .'

I was about to say that I really liked him though, when she interrupted.

'Good, I'm glad you don't, because when he came over to clear away our glasses I asked him if he was just working here for the holidays, and he said, "Dunno," so I said, "Are you going back to school in September?" and he said, "Not really sure yet." Then I said, "What will you do if you don't go back?" and he said, "Dunno really." So I thought, *You're on to a loser here, Claire*. And I shut up.'

Claire's voice had sounded as though she was really taking the rip out of Robby, and again, for some unknown reason, I felt like sticking up for him.

'I think he's just shy,' I said for the second time that day. 'But he *is* really nice, you know.'

'Well, I reckon he's a total dweeb . . .'

I didn't like Claire calling him that, but she'd changed the subject before I could reply and was on about the history homework.

When we hung up I went into the sitting room. Jon and Alex were there and they both begged me to join in their game. They wouldn't leave me alone, no matter how often I told them I was tired and I didn't feel like playing their pathetic games.

'Oh go on, Bethany, it's more fun with three,' whined Jon.

'I've said no about a hundred times, Jon. Now go away and leave me in peace.'

But the stupid kid still kept on. 'Just for one game then we'll leave you alone.'

'Look, I'll tell Mum about the vase if you don't go away,' I finally said, because I knew this was the one thing that would get through to him.

But I was wrong.

'I'll just tell her you made it up, and she'll believe me because that man's obviously forgotten all about it by now. That's what *you* said.'

'Well, I was only saying that to stop you worrying your guts out about your dad finding out. You may as well know that my mum had a right go at me, *and* she told Anne, and that's why I'm working at the café – to pay it back. So there, know-all!'

If only I'd kept my mouth shut at that moment. But I didn't, and I had no idea just how badly my words would backfire.

11 THE MASSIVE SHOCK

It was weird because it felt as though I'd been working at Ric's for weeks, but it was only my second time.

Louisa and Kerry had gone out with Kerry's family on a shopping trip, so Claire came in on her own. She grabbed my arm as I passed her table.

'I've just seen Guy,' she whispered. 'He was on the Ten Items Or Less checkout, looking gorgeous in one of those grey jackets!' I couldn't help giggling. 'I reckon you might fancy one of his mates,' she went on. 'They don't go red every two seconds and they're not at all dweeby.'

She rolled her eyes towards the counter where Robby was making cappuccinos.

'He's not dweeby,' I said, defending him. 'I told you, he's shy.'

'Whatever,' said Claire, getting up and giving me the money for her Coke. 'Anyway, I'll give you a ring later.'

I took the money (all in coppers – typical Claire!) over to Robby who was at the till, then went to take an order for a couple at table six. I heard the jangle of money hitting the floor and turned round to see a red-faced Robby bending down to pick up the coins he'd dropped.

'Three coffees,' said the man at table four. But he might as well have been talking Martian, because I didn't take it in, I was so gobsmacked by the sight of Robby's face. It had gone from bright red to chalk white in seconds. He was staring at the door. Then he suddenly bolted into the kitchen, nearly knocking Sue over as she came through to the café.

I looked over to see what ever could have given him such a scare. Then I got one too because Mum and Colin were coming through the door. I started to panic and felt as though *I* should have been the one bolting into the kitchen, and yet I didn't know why I was feeling like that. After all, Anne had told Mum that I was working in the café on Saturdays, so there was no reason for me to feel worried.

'Did you get that?'

'Sorry . . . what?'

The man whose order I was taking was looking at me as though I was a hopeless case.

'Three coffees,' he said loudly, in case I was deaf as well as thick.

And that's when two things happened. Mum caught sight of me and gave me a bright smile.

And I suddenly realised why I'd felt panicky – I was only standing there with gold studs in my ears, wasn't I?

'Three coffees,' I echoed vacantly, then I shot off to the kitchen too.

'Omigod, I've got to get these studs out right now!' I said to Robby. There was no point in talking to Adrian because he'd got his back to me and he was always surrounded by so many hissing, splattering, whirring noises that he could never hear what anyone was saying.

'Here, I'll help you,' said Robby.

'That's my mum out there!' I blurted out.

I could feel his fingers trembling on my right ear, and I suddenly thought, *This is weird. He's in just as bad a state as I am.*

'I guessed that.'

I swung round because he'd totally surprised me. And in that instant we both heard the tiny sound of one of my studs hitting the floor. 'You guessed? How?'

'Because I kind of worked it out.'

'You worked it out?'

I knew I must have sounded moronic, but I didn't get where he was coming from.

'Yeah, because I heard that kid call you Bethany, that time when he came crashing in to say that Jon had broken the vase. And I thought there can't be that many Jons and Bethanys who are brother and sister in this place.'

'But . . . I don't get you. What if we *are* called Jon and Bethany?'

He was bending down, looking for my stud, so I couldn't see his face.

'Well . . . I know your mum, you see . . .'

'You know my mum? How?'

'Because – oh, here it is!'

He was holding up the missing stud. 'Thanks,' I said, as I took it from him. But his hand was trembling. There was something weird going on, but I couldn't work out what it was. 'How do you know my mum?'

'Because she's my stepmother.'

I stared at him for ages, while my brain slowly put the facts together. And once I'd clicked what he meant, the shock made me lean against the wall for support, otherwise I might have keeled over. 'So Colin is your dad . . .'

He nodded.

But it still wasn't making sense. 'But Mum calls you Alisdair . . .'

'That's my name – Alisdair Robinson – only everyone calls me Robby. Well, everyone except Dad, Kathy, my mum and my stepfather.'

I gulped and stared at him all goggle-eyed as though he'd changed into a toad or something. Then I gulped again as I remembered who was out there in the café.

'So why don't you want your dad and my

mum to see you?' I managed to whisper.

'Because they think I work in a smart financial services place called Townley's, not a café.'

'That's right, they do!' I gasped as Sue came into the kitchen.

'Are you all right, you two?' she said. 'You both look as though you've seen a ghost.'

'Robby's not feeling well,' I blurted out. 'And my studs are really hurting. I think it's because I keep forgetting to put that stuff on them at night. I'm just taking them out.'

'Sit down for a bit, Robby. I'll get you a glass of water.'

I felt for the little butterfly at the back of my other ear. 'I'll do Robby's orders until he feels better,' I added, feeling my ear getting hotter.

'Ooh!' said Sue, wrinkling her nose. 'I shouldn't take them out if I were you. Not till the five weeks are up. The holes will seal up and then you'll have to do them again.'

'I'll just keep them out till I finish work. I don't think they'll seal up in that short time.'

'Well, we'd better get a wriggle on,' said Sue. 'Sophie's holding the fort out there. But don't you worry, Robby. The lunchtime rush is over.'

And with that she dashed back into the café. There were so many questions I wanted to ask Robby, but I couldn't because I had to get back to work. And I knew that even if I had all the time in the world, I wouldn't be able to find the answers, because I simply didn't know what the questions were. It was all so weird. One minute I know this bloke called Robby and I really like him, and I don't know my stepbrother, Alisdair, but from what I've heard, I don't think I'm going to like him. And now my brain doesn't know which way to turn, because Robby *is* Alisdair. But which is the *real* Alisdair? And do

I like him? And why, *why* has he told my mum and Colin that he works at Townley's when he doesn't?

There were all these questions jostling for space in my mind, and what's the one question I ask? 'Do the holes show?'

He looked carefully. 'Pull a bit more hair out on this side.'

So I pulled out an extra little strand. 'That's better. Your ears look a bit red, that's all.'

Then he sighed an enormous sigh, which made the questions come rushing to my lips. But there wasn't time now. I gave him what was supposed to be an encouraging smile. 'I'll take Mum and Colin's order straight away. The sooner they get started, the sooner they'll leave.'

The moment I went back into the café and approached the dreaded table, my heart started pounding.

'I've done that one,' whispered Sue, when she

saw where I was heading. 'Take number four's order.'

Saved!

I tried to keep as far away as possible from their table, and every so often I took a quick glance over. The first couple of times they weren't looking, thank goodness, but the third time, Mum was smiling at me. If only I wasn't so worried about my earlobes showing, I would have felt really pleased with myself, because it looked like Mum was quite proud of her daughter being a waitress. I flashed her a quick smile, which probably came out like a terrible grimace, because I was so worried that she'd spot the holes in my earlobes. And maybe I was imagining it, but it felt like their eyes were following me around the café as I served people and took orders. So it was a big relief every time I had to go through to the kitchen.

Robby was just sitting there trying to look ill,

but only succeeding in looking really hacked off.

I took a deep breath. 'Would your dad be cross if he knew you worked here?'

He nodded glumly, and murmured, 'Uh-huh.'

It reminded me of when Claire told me that she'd asked him all those questions about school and holidays and work and everything and he'd just given one-word answers. Claire had called him a dweeb. It was so obvious she didn't think much of him.

My heart started hammering because I'd suddenly realised I was going to have to tell her – in fact tell everyone – that quiet, red-faced, shy Robby was actually my stepbrother. How was I going to break this great news? *Oh, by the way, you know Robby? Well, actually it turns out that not only is he a dweeb but he's also my stepbrother! Brilliant, isn't it?*

I looked at him, sitting there all pale. Surely things couldn't be as bad as he was making out? 'Mum and Colin don't seem to mind that *I'm* working here.'

'You're different,' was all he managed to mumble. 'I feel terrible sitting here when I should be working. Can you see if they've nearly finished.'

'No time for chatter, Bethany,' said Sue, looking highly frazzled as she swung into the kitchen. 'How are you feeling, Robby? You've got a bit of colour back now.'

'Still a bit funny,' said Robby.

Sue didn't say anything to that – just grabbed some scones that Adrian had buttered and rushed back out again, so I followed her.

As I went to serve drinks at the counter, I took a discreet glance to see how much gooey cake was left on Mum and Colin's plates. Hardly any. Good.

But then Mum beckoned me over. I pretended to pick something up off the floor and while I was bending down I pulled two massive chunks of hair out of my pony tail and made sure they were completely covering my ears.

'We'll be off in a mo, love,' she said, speaking quickly so as not to waste my time. 'We only just popped in to see how you were getting on.'

'Oh. Right,' I said, standing back in case she tried to tuck my hair back or something.

Then Mum screwed her face up as though she was in pain and said, 'It's such a shame that you haven't met Alisdair yet, though. He's gone off on his own again. Maybe once he's met you, you can introduce him to some young people . . .'

'I think Bethany's friends will be a bit too young,' said Colin, flapping his hand, as though my friends went to playgroup. 'I've told him often enough, he should get in with the local cricket team, or do something worthwhile like that, instead of wasting his time on photos.'

Colin was clearly not impressed. I didn't know what to say, but I couldn't help feeling sorry for Robby.

'I'd better get on. I'll give you a ring tomorrow, OK?'

'No, I'll ring *you*. In fact, if Alisdair is around we'll pop over.'

So I went to give someone their bill, and then I took an order. And by the time I was going back to the kitchen they were just leaving.

'Hallelujah!' I said to Robby. 'They've gone at last!'

'Thank goodness!' he said. Then he rushed through to the café.

For the rest of the afternoon I got myself more and more screwed up about what I was going to say to Claire and the others. Then I made myself cross because it shouldn't matter what I said. He's my stepbrother and that's the end of that. There's nothing anyone can do about it. The trouble is, part of me feels a bit embarrassed about him and another part feels sorry for him. And then there's another part that simply doesn't get him. I mean, he's sixteen, for God's sake! What's the big deal about working in a café? Why did he have to make up that he was working in some wonderful financial set-up?

I knew I'd never find the answers to all my questions during work, because there wasn't time. But I was determined to tackle him about it afterwards.

12 THE INQUISITION

I finished work before Robby, but I hung about drinking tea in the kitchen and talking to Adrian while I waited. Then at half-past five we set off walking home together. I knew I'd have to get on to *the* conversation straight away, because at Caryon Lane, he'd go one way and I'd go the other.

'I don't get why you're so worried about what your dad'll say if he finds out you work in the café. I mean, what's wrong with the café?'

'Nothing. It's a great place to work. But he won't see it like that. And . . .'

'What?'

'Doesn't matter.'

There was something about the way his face had closed up that stopped me from asking any more. I knew I'd be puzzling over it afterwards though.

'Mum's trying to get you and me to meet each other tomorrow,' I said, grinning at him. 'That's a laugh, isn't it?'

He shook his head as though the world had gone mad and he was the only sane person left in it. 'Actually, I was going to go to . . . but it doesn't matter.'

'Where? Where were you going to go? Mum and Colin said you often go off on your own.'

He looked at me sharply. 'Did they say anything else?'

I somehow didn't think he'd appreciate what

Colin had said about his photos or about joining the cricket team. 'Not really. So what do you do when you go off to places?'

'Look at stuff ... walk ... take photos. I don't mind being on my own. There's no pressure.'

I was imagining him wandering around all alone. It was quite a sad thought. But then a bigger thought drowned that one.

'Omigod!'

'What?'

'I've left my earrings at the café. I'm so stupid. They're just lying around in the kitchen.'

'Don't worry, I put them both in the drawer where the tea towels are kept.'

'The holes in my ears are going to completely close up now,' I wailed.

'Couldn't you buy some more? I'll lend you the money.'

'But everywhere's shut. It's after five-thirty.'

He frowned and tapped his chin thoughtfully, while I looked at him, and thought, *This is so weird. I'm walking along with my stepbrother.*

'I've got it!' he said, stopping suddenly. 'We go to Claire's house right now and you ask if you can borrow her studs till Monday after school. Then you go down to the café and collect your own. I'll make sure they're safe during Monday. Then we can have a drink together because I finish at four on Mondays.'

I felt like giving him a big hug for coming up with such a wicked plan, but I couldn't, because I was still too confused about him.

'That's brilliant, Robby,' I said instead.

'Well, come on then. Let's get going. Where does she live?'

And that was when I realised that there was a flaw in his great plan, because I couldn't go whizzing up to Claire's front door with Robby in tow. It'd be too embarrassing for words. Her eyes might pop out of her head when I announced that *this* was my stepbrother. And one thing I didn't want was for Claire to feel sorry for me. If only she still thought he was really cool, like she did when she first wanted me to meet him. I'd have to try and convince her that he wasn't a dweeb at all. And for that I'd need plenty of time. I'd break it to her gently one day at school next week. Yes, that's what I'd do.

'It's all right – I'll just go on my own.'

'No, I'll come with you. I'm not in any hurry to get home, and we can talk for longer.'

'But what if someone sees us?'

He looked at me with such a bewildered face, I nearly took a rain check on that hugging thing.

'No – I mean, what if your mum and Colin saw us? There'd be all sorts of questions to answer.'

'Yeah, maybe you're right.'

Phew!

I let myself in through the back door and knew instantly that something was wrong, because I could hear that Anne was in the kitchen, and yet she didn't call out to me.

I tried to sound normal but my heart was beating like mad. 'Hi, Anne.'

'Hello,' she replied. But it wasn't her usual voice.

Either she'd found out that Mum knew nothing about the earrings, or Mum had found about the vase and she'd told Anne. Either way, things were not looking good. I thought about going straight upstairs, but it was probably better to face the music.

'We realised we'd completely run out of loo paper a little while ago,' said Anne, looking at me as though I was personally responsible. *I mean*, loo paper? *Where was this conversation going?* 'So Dad went into town to get some more, and on his way home he passed a boy and a girl deep in conversation, and when he looked through his driving mirror he was quite surprised to see it was you and a much older looking boy.'

I couldn't work out what her problem was at first. Then I realised she was worried that I was secretly going out with someone and he was way too old for me.

'But that was Robby – you know, the boy who works at the café.'

'Ah.' Anne looked happier now. 'So not a boyfriend then?'

'No, of course not.'

'OK, but . . .' Her voice went low, '. . . but it was at least half an hour ago when Dad passed you. Where have you been since then?'

'I went round to Claire's. She left something

at the café on Friday, and I was just giving it back.'

Anne nodded, but I had the feeling there was more to come. 'The other thing I'm trying to get to the bottom of –' *Here we go* '– is some problem or other that Jon and Alex have got involved with.' *Oh no! Whatever have those stupid boys being saying?* 'I had a phone call from Mrs Trent just down the road here earlier on. She was asking me in a rather embarrassed tone of voice if I knew that Jon and Alex were going round knocking on people's doors and asking if they could wash their cars for them.'

I gasped. Dad came into the kitchen at that moment.

He managed to say hello to me through tight lips, but Anne immediately told him that it was OK because the boy he'd seen me with was only Robby who works in the café. Dad looked a bit less tense then – but only a bit.

Anne carried on. 'I've just given the boys a massive lecture on dangers and strangers, and they're both feeling full of remorse. That's why you can't hear a sound from them. They're watching telly at the moment. But –' I had the feeling the punch line was coming, and the look on Dad's face made me even more sure – 'Alex happened to say that they were only washing cars so they could earn money to give to you, Bethany, because they felt sorry for you.' She looked me straight in the eye. 'Now, what do you suppose he meant by that?'

This was terrible. The trouble was, I didn't know how much the boys had actually confessed. I didn't want to tell any lies if they'd told the truth. I'd just be digging a big hole for myself if I did that. I shrugged – a sort of sorry, can't-help-you shrug.

Dad's voice was so cold I hardly recognised it. 'Nothing to say, Bethany?'

So now it was an inquisition, was it?

'I think . . . they thought I had to pay for my own studs.'

'Hm.'

What did that *mean?*

'Let's go and find out. Come on,' said Anne.

I was marched through to the sitting room, Anne in front, Dad behind. It was like they were actually enjoying the build-up to the big showdown. My whole body went into tense mode and my heart sounded like a drum kit.

John and Alex were sitting at either end of the settee. They both looked round at the sound of Anne's brisk entrance. Then, when they saw me following stiffly behind, their eyes shot back to the TV screen.

Anne grabbed the control quite roughly and flicked it towards the telly. Then we were left with not a sound to dull the pain of the torture. 'I want to get to the bottom of the reason why you two have been trying to earn money,' she said, hands on hips, eyes smouldering.

I saw Alex wince. The poor kid was supposed to be staying the night at our place. I bet he was wishing he could go home.

'It wasn't Bethany's fault,' he said, big eyes on me.

Great start, Alex. Do we have *to talk about faults?*

'*What* wasn't Bethany's fault, Alex?' asked Dad.

Jon sat up abruptly. 'It *was* her fault. She was supposed to be looking after us.'

I may as well shoot myself and get it over with.

'When?' Anne asked.

'That time when you and Mike went to the garden centre.'

Anne was looking intently at Jon. 'Yes . . . so you and Alex were on your own . . . and what happened?'

Jon's shoulders rose about five centimetres, and he stayed like that – all tense, thinking about his dad, I guess. 'Nothing.'

'Jon broke a glass vase in the gift shop,' blurted out Alex, who obviously wanted to get this whole thing out in the open, bless him. (*Not.*)

Anne's eyes widened and her mouth fell open. I didn't look at Dad.

'We were in the café, right?' I started gabbling. 'And we'd hardly sat down when Jon wanted to go and spend his pocket money.'

'Huh! That's not true!' said Jon, going red in the face. 'We'd been there ages.'

'No, we hadn't!' I snapped, hating myself for sinking to Jon's pathetic, argumentative little level. 'I just wanted a quiet drink with my friends. It's not much to ask, is it?'

'You never did!' Jon shouted. 'You only wanted to stay there for ages because you fancy that waiter.'

'No, she doesn't,' said Alex, trying desperately to defend his idol. 'She only likes him because he was nice to her when she hurt her ankle.'

'That's rubbish!' said Jon. 'She fancies him. It's so obvious. Even a blind person'd be able to tell. So there.'

Oh, thanks very much, Jon. This means death.

I stared at the carpet. Anne was glaring at me. I could feel her eyes boring holes in my face. The room was wrapped in this awful silence. I felt like screaming out, 'Look, Robby isn't Robby – he's Alisdair!'

But I couldn't, because it would only make things even more complicated, because then Anne might worry that I was having a secret relationship with my stepbrother, and she'd call up Mum in a big panic and then Alisdair would be in double trouble.

So I kept my mouth shut and my eyes on the carpet.

'How much did the vase cost?' Anne asked softly.

'Thirty-five pounds,' Alex told her in a shaky voice.

'Which gift shop?'

'Kellet's.'

'And what did the shopkeeper say?'

I knew Jon would freak out if I said that the shopkeeper seemed to have forgotten all about it, and I just made it up that I owed him thirty-five pounds. I had to think quickly here.

'Can we talk in the kitchen?' I asked Anne.

Without a word she turned and marched out of the room. Again I followed her meekly and Dad brought up the rear.

'I *thought* I was going to have to pay for it because the shopkeeper asked for my parents' phone number, and I gave him Mum's because Jon was scared that if you found out, you might tell his dad. I guess the boys were feeling guilty or something. That's why they decided to try and help me out. But I had no idea they were doing car washing, honestly.'

'I'll go and see the man at Kellet's on Monday and sort it out. I'm not particularly happy about it, because I just wish you'd both come home and told the truth straight away.'

'But you would have been cross about me letting the boys go off on their own, and they were getting on my nerves.'

'What *I'm* most concerned about, Bethany, is that there appears to be something going on between you and this young man who works at the café,' said Dad.

'I promise there isn't.'

'You promise?'

'Promise.'

They both gave me a searching look. I tried not to go red. I really tried.

13 BUILDING UP THE BIG LIE

All through school on Monday I tried to make myself tell Claire that Robby was actually my stepbrother, but somehow I just couldn't get the words out of my mouth. She wouldn't stop talking about Guy, and she'd got it into her head that it would be a great idea if I got to meet his friends, then I was sure to fancy one of them.

'They're so much cooler than Robby, Beth, honestly.'

After school I walked down to the café on my own. Louisa and Kerry had art club, and Claire had gone home to get changed so she could impress Guy. I'd told them all I was going to collect my studs. That was true, of course, but now it wasn't so important as talking to Robby. I'd done nothing but think about him all through Sunday. There was still so much I wanted to ask him.

He was sitting at one of the tables when I went in. He'd actually ordered me a Coke and a cake. This was unbelievable. It was like we were meeting on a date. Thank goodness I wasn't with Claire. It might have been just a touch hard to explain.

'Here are your earrings,' he said, the moment I sat down.

'Thanks, Robby.' I started tucking into my cake because I'm always starving after school. 'Why *do* you call yourself Robby, anyway? Don't you like Alisdair?'

'My friends all call me Robby. Even my teachers do. It's my nickname. Like I said, it's only the parents who call me Alisdair.' His face looked suddenly dark. 'I can't say that I like Alisdair very much – especially when my stepdad says it in his heavy accent.'

I felt as though he was trying to tell me something important here. 'So you don't like your stepdad?'

He shook his head and I stuffed more cake into my mouth because I didn't know what to say next.

'I came to live with Dad and Kathy to get away from him – *and* Mum. She's nearly as bad.'

'What, you mean strict?'

He was folding and refolding the napkin on his lap, his chin practically on his chest. It was like someone had put a gun to his head and said, '*You've got to fold this napkin small enough to fit through a keyhole or you're dead.'*

'You could say that.'

I felt so sorry for him. I stopped eating cake, pushed the plate away and leaned forwards. He suddenly tugged the napkin a couple of times and put it on the table. I couldn't help gasping. He'd made a frog out of it. It looked so realistic.

'That's brilliant, Robby!'

'I like doing stuff like that.'

'You're so clever!'

'No, I'm not. I've had God knows how much money spent on my private education, I've had loads of extra tuition, I'm expected to get ten A stars for GCSE and I'm supposed to do something equally stunning at A level, and then they expect me to invent something that'll change the world before I leave university. But changing the world isn't what I want to do. I just want to do my own thing – like wait in cafés, take photos and make stupid frogs out of paper napkins. Only that's not good enough for them, as they keep ramming down my throat every ten seconds. And why isn't it? Because of all the money they've put into my education. It all comes back to that.'

I didn't speak, I just stared at him. I couldn't believe what I was hearing. Talk about cruel parents!

'You've got cake crumbs all over your face,' Robby said, in a matter-of-fact voice.

I didn't seem to have a napkin, and nearly grabbed the frog to wipe my mouth, but I couldn't bear to ruin such a work of art so I leaned back and took a napkin from the next table.

'No wonder you wanted to come down here and live with your real dad and my mum.'

'Yeah. I had to convince Mum and my stepdad that I'd find a really high-powered job down here. That was the only way they'd agree to it.'

'Didn't they want you to come?'

'No. My mum's quite jealous of your mum, and over the years she's practically lost touch with my dad. And because of never seeing him, I'd lost touch too. But then my stepdad got dead keen on me working at what he called a proper job, and he reckoned there were more job opportunities in England, so that's when Mum got in touch with Dad.

'When I first came down here and told Dad that I'd probably get a job in a shop or a café or something, he went spare, and said that he hadn't been forking out for all these years to give me a good education so I could work in a shop. On and on and on – I tell you it does my head in.'

'But who actually pays for your education? Your mum or your dad?'

'It's hard to say. Dad pays Mum maintenance money. My stepdad's got a good job. My mum's got some inheritance money. They all think I should be really grateful to them. But my stepdad's the worst. He acts like I'm a massive drain on his life.'

'Doesn't he . . . like you?'

'He takes it out on me because his own two children – Hannah and Craig – live miles away and aren't interested in seeing him. In fact they've got their own stepdad, and they get on really well with him.'

'No wonder you hid in the kitchen when Mum and Colin came in here on Saturday.'

He gave me a half-smile, and shrugged. Then he looked suddenly worried. 'Don't tell your mum, whatever you do.'

'But you can't go on like this. It's not fair. You've got to be yourself, and tell them – tell them where to shove their private education.'

'It's easy to say, Bethany.'

'Yeah. Sorry.'

'All I know is that when I have kids of my own, I'm going to make sure they're happy, and I'm not going to expect them to do well at everything.'

'What about cleaning round the bath?' I couldn't help asking, with a grin.

'Pathetic, isn't it? I just don't want to be any trouble to Dad and Kathy, otherwise they might send me packing. And I like it down here. I've taken some great photos . . . and I've met my stepsister.'

Now *I* was the one blushing.

'Can I see some of your photos?' I asked him.

'You probably won't like them.'

'Try me,' I said, feeling suddenly very curious.

He'd got a small rucksack with him and he pulled out an orange envelope. 'These are the latest ones.'

He laid twelve photos out over the table. I looked from one to the other carefully. They were nearly all the same. It was the sea in the background – or was it the sky? I couldn't tell. And in the foreground was a kind of fountain.

'This is lovely . . . this one,' I said. 'You've made the fountain look like sparkling glitter, and the sky is all in layers.'

Then my eye scanned across the others. 'Oh, it's not a fountain – it's tree! Wow! That's clever!' I peered more closely at the background in all the photos. 'Oh! It's not the sky either! It's the sea.'

When I looked up at him he was nearly smiling.

'It's the sea *and* the sky. I went to Gore Beach and waited for low tide because I wanted to play around with the light and the horizon. I lay on my stomach on a sand dune . . .'

I looked at him sitting there, making another

frog out of my crumby napkin as he stared at one of the photos through half-shut eyes, and I thought how clever he was.

'Fancy Mum preferring old churches to this!' I said, shaking my head.

He laughed and gathered up the photos in one swift move. 'She's not the only one who feels that way. Which reminds me, we're all coming round Friday night so I can "meet" you. Hope you're a good actress.'

I didn't say anything, but I was thinking that actually it would just be another part of the great big lie.

When I got back from the café, Anne was wearing her unimpressed look. She greeted me with her head on one side and her arms folded.

'I went down to Kellet's today and had a word with the owner there.'

I gulped and waited, with my heart in overdrive.

'Apparently a tall, good-looking young man knocked on the shop door when they'd just closed, on the day Jon broke the vase. And this young man paid the thirty-five pounds in cash. Just like that!'

Robby! It had to be Robby. Through my head flashed a picture of what had happened that afternoon. Alex had come crashing back into the café, all white-faced, to tell me what had happened. He'd called out 'Bethany' and he'd said the name 'Jon'. Robby had already told me he'd made the connection, but he never said he'd paid for the vase out of his own money, to get his stepsister out of trouble.

And now Mum was glaring at me, because she thought she'd got even more proof that I was going out with the boy who worked in the café. What a mess! If only I could tell her the truth. But I couldn't. Grown-ups stick together on these things. She'd tell my mum instantly.

'I'm – I'm paying him back. He was just doing me a favour because I told him you'd be really cross.'

'Promise?'

Not this again.

'Promise.'

14 BREAKING DOWN
THE BIG LIE

For the rest of the week I tried to pluck up courage to tell Claire that Robby was my stepbrother. I nearly managed it on Tuesday. I got as far as telling her that Robby had been a big hero and paid for the vase. I thought she'd be impressed by that. But no. She'd gasped all right, but then when I'd been on the point of announcing that the hero was actually my stepbrother, she'd suddenly said, 'What a sucker. I mean, very nice for you and all that. But it's not exactly normal, is it?'

So then I didn't have the guts to deliver the punch line, so I just kept quiet and put it off till the next day, then the next, then the next.

And then it was Friday after school, and Claire and I were on our way to Ric's. This was my very last chance. Claire hadn't been to the café at all during the week because she'd been walking home via the supermarket. But today she was actually meeting Golden Boy Guy at Ric's and she wanted me to come with her because he might have one of his friends with him.

Robby was sure to assume that I would have told Claire that he was my long-lost stepbrother. He might say something to her about it, when he served her and Guy. And then I'd feel absolutely terrible, because how would I be able to explain why I hadn't even told my best friend this big news? Poor Robby would think I was ashamed of him. I was kicking myself for not having had the guts to say anything all week.

And now I was down to my last few minutes.
And I didn't even want to go to Ric's to meet
Guy's friend.

'I wonder if Robby's working today,' Claire
suddenly said.

*This is your chance. Speak, Bethany! Just open
your mouth and speak!*

'Yeah. And talking of Robby . . . you know I
told you how he paid for that vase?'

She looked at me sharply. My voice must
have given away my nervousness.

'Yeah.'

'Well, there's a reason why he did that.' I
could tell I'd got her interested. I just wished
she'd stop walking quite so fast. We'd be there
in a few seconds. 'You see . . .' I was going for
the loudest recorded heartbeat ever '. . . he's my
stepbrother.'

There, I'd said it. Nothing had happened.
The world hadn't stopped. I was walking in

through the café door and Claire – wait a sec, where *was* Claire? I turned round. She was standing, rooted to the spot where I'd made my announcement a few metres up the road.

'Why didn't you tell me?' she screeched, coming back to earth and staggering up to me as though the shock had made her legs go wobbly.

'Because you went on and on about what a dweeb he was, and all that. What do you expect?'

'Shut the door,' said Sue a bit snappily. 'There's a draught.'

Robby was just coming through from the kitchen. He gave me a wink and walked over. Claire looked from one to the other of us, as though we'd both sprouted a horn in the middle of our foreheads, and I'd just informed her we were actually a pair of unicorns posing as human beings.

'I didn't expect to see you here today,' said Robby.

It was on the tip of my tongue to thank him for paying for the vase, but I decided it would only embarrass him and make him go pink, so I kept quiet about it.

'I just popped in to say hi, as I haven't had the chance to see you since Monday.'

'Yeah, but it's the official introduction later, remember. Whatever you do, don't forget to call me Alisdair.'

I nodded and giggled nervously. Claire was still looking from one to the other of us, her jaw hanging open.

Glancing round, I saw two boys sitting at the corner table, grinning in our direction. 'I take it that's Guy's over there,' I said, giving her a gentle shove to get her going in the right direction. 'Sorry, can't stay after all. I'll phone you later.'

Then, as Claire wandered off to the corner

table like a zombie in shock, I said 'bye to Robby and made a quick exit.

'Looking forward to meeting Alisdair?' were Anne's first words as I went into the kitchen.

I shrugged as though I wasn't bothered one way or the other. Then something hit me right between the eyes and I didn't know why on earth I hadn't thought about it before. *Jon*. Jon would recognise Robby, wouldn't he? I had to talk to him quickly and try to get it into his thick skull that he must *not*, under any circumstances, let on that Robby worked in the café.

'Where's Jon?'

'At a party. They've gone bowling at the complex and then for a McDonald's.'

Oh no! 'What time is he getting back?'

'Seven or eight. Can't remember. Have you had a good day?'

'Not bad . . .'

This was disastrous. It couldn't have been worse. I'd just have to listen like mad, and the moment I heard a car pull up outside, I'd go belting out to brief him. Right. Sorted. But hang on a sec – Jon wasn't the only one who might recognise Robby.

'When's Dad getting back?'

'He's going to be really late tonight. He'll have to meet Alisdair another time.'

Phew! At least I didn't have to worry about that one.

'What time are they coming round?'

'Er . . . some time between six and seven. I've had a big tidy-up. Crazy, isn't it, tidying up for a sixteen-year-old boy? But I've been led to believe that he's so organised and smart, and I don't want him to think his stepsister lives in a total tip!'

I wished I could tell Anne that she needn't

have bothered about tidying up, because Alisdair wouldn't really care. In fact, he'd probably prefer it messy.

It was a quarter to seven when they turned up. I was a bag of nerves by then. Anne answered the door.

'Hello, darling,' said Mum, rushing forwards and giving me a hug. She turned round and beckoned Alisdair to join her. I tried to imagine I'd never set eyes on him before, but it was impossible and in the end it was easier to look at the carpet. Unfortunately he was doing the same thing.

'Alisdair, meet Bethany.'

Anne must taken my peculiar behaviour for embarrassment, because she started giving me little jobs to do. 'Can you get the tray of glasses from the kitchen, Beth, and I'll get the nibbles. Do go in and sit down, Kathy. Make yourselves at home. We'll only be two seconds.'

'Need any help, Anne?' asked Colin.

'No, no, I've got my young waitress here, remember?'

'Yes, of course,' smiled Mum. 'We've seen her in action in the café, and I must say we were very impressed.'

A few minutes later we were all sitting round with drinks and nibbles, as the adults called them, which made me feel like a hamster.

'I hear you work at Townley's,' said Anne, smiling at Alisdair.

Oh no! This was the very subject Robby wanted to avoid. I'd better change the conversation quickly. Without weighing up the consequences I 'accidentally' knocked my plate out of my hand, making my sausage roll go flying through the air and land plonk in Colin's lap, as though I'd done it on purpose.

Robby let out a spurt of laughter.

'Sorry!' I said, diving across the room and grabbing it back. Anne looked as though she was about to burst into giggles, and so did Mum. But Colin was clearly not amused. Bits of pastry dropped off all over the place. 'Sorry,' I repeated.

'I'm surprised you're not rushing to Bethany's assistance, Alisdair,' said Mum with a twinkle in her eye.

I went to get the brush and dustpan, and a moment later I was back in time to hear her say, 'This is honestly the tidiest boy you've ever met, Anne. I shall be sorry to see him go.'

'Oh, when *are* you going?' Anne asked Robby.

'I'm not sure yet . . .' mumbled Robby.

'Have you got the job at Townley's for the whole holiday period?' Anne went on.

Robby went red again and nodded.

'He's so modest,' said Mum, 'isn't he, Colin?'

'You're embarrassing the poor boy,' said Colin.

Then the very worst thing that could possibly happen, happened. The door opened and in rushed Jon. 'I won! It was so wicked! You should have seen me –' Then he stopped because he'd spotted Robby. I closed my eyes and prepared for the worst. 'What are you doing here, Robby?'

Mum and Colin exchanged a puzzled glance, then raised their eyebrows at Anne.

'Do you know Alisdair, Jon?' asked Anne.

'Alisdair?' said Jon, pulling a face, as though Anne had got a few screws loose. 'This isn't Alisdair. It's Robby. He works at the café . . .'

Then, seeing the blank disbelief on the adults' faces, Jon turned to me. 'Doesn't he, Bethy?'

I nodded slowly, and the silence filled every corner of the room.

'I'm just getting a drink of water,' said Jon quietly.

The moment he'd gone out, Colin turned to Robby. 'Is this true?' he asked in a low voice.

Robby nodded.

Mum's eyes widened. 'You mean, you haven't been working at Townley's?'

Robby shook his head.

He didn't look worried. He didn't look anything.

I felt as though I was holding my breath, waiting for a massive row to start. Anne looked like that too.

'Why did you deliberately lie to us?' asked Colin in an ice-cold voice that was quivering with rage.

Robby took a deep breath. I thought he was about to speak, but he just let it out again.

'You know very well your mother and step-father were expecting you to get a proper job,' Mum said, in a gentler tone.

But I'd suddenly had enough. How dared they make poor Robby's life so difficult! He couldn't even answer back because he was a guest in someone else's house. But *I* wasn't. A big temper was working its way up from my feet. I jumped up as it reached my mouth. Then out it raged.

'What is your problem, you two? Robby *had* to lie. Everyone expects so much of him, just because he's been to private school. Have you ever asked him what *he* wants to do? I've only met him a few times and already I know him better than you two!' I practically screamed at Mum and Colin.

Colin just ignored me, as though I was a hysterical little girl. And that really bugged me.

'Why didn't you tell us, Alisdair? There was no need to lie, was there?' he asked, trying to sound all reasonable.

I was about to start yelling again, when Robby calmly said, 'Yes, there was, actually. You see, I can't *tell* you anything – just like I can't *tell* the other two parents anything. I've been brought up not to do the *telling*. I'm expected to do as I'm *told*. "Go to private school, Alisdair, and make sure you do well in all your exams, because we're paying big bucks for this, Alisdair. Take sciences, Alisdair. That's what universities want these days – scientists. Or what about maths, Alisdair? Then you can go into the money markets. That's where you want to be, Alisdair. In the money markets."' His voice rose. 'But maybe I don't want to take sciences. Maybe I'd prefer to take photos. Did anyone think of that?'

'Photos!' said Colin, with a sneer in his voice.

'Yeah, photos,' I said, raising my voice. 'They're brilliant. You should see them.'

'The point is, nobody's ever actually asked me what *I* want to do,' said Robby.

'Hold on a minute,' said Colin, his voice still ice-cold. 'I don't think you realise how much money we've forked out for your education over the years. It's all for your own good, you know.'

'But how do you know what's good for me, when you don't even ask?'

Colin turned to Mum and shook his head, as though they'd got a right case on their hands here. 'I can't believe that this is all the thanks we get, Kathy.'

I swallowed and looked at Robby. Then I got a shock. He slowly leaned forwards and eyeballed Colin. 'Sorry, I didn't realise you were expecting thanks.'

Colin blinked and looked more furious than ever. Mum was biting her lip and looking very pale. Anne's eyes were flashing, but I couldn't tell what she was thinking.

'Is that all you have to say?' asked Colin.

'I'd say a lot more if I thought there was a chance that you might listen,' said Robby, getting up. 'But if you won't listen, maybe you'll look.'

And with that he tipped up his rucksack so loads of packs of photos fell on to the floor. Then he calmly walked out. And I followed him.

Just before I closed the door behind me I met Anne's eyes. They were bright with tears . . . and something else. She gave me the smallest of winks, and I knew she was on Robby's and my side. I guessed she was thinking exactly what I was thinking. 'Yessssss!'

15 A GREAT TEAM

I'm at Ric's clearing tables and taking orders on autopilot. For the last hour and a half I've been working like a zombie, my mind going over the events of last night. But every so often Robby's eyes meet mine and we exchange a look that no one would begin to understand. Looking back on yesterday evening is like going back over a dream that was very vivid but has begun to fade. Most of all I remember what Robby said to me the moment we'd walked out on the adults.

'I know it sounds dramatic but I feel free

now. I don't have to lie because I don't care what anyone says any more.'

We walked for ages, Robby and I. He thanked me for defending him. I said it was no big deal. But it was. Sticking up for him like that had made me change my mind about so much stuff. Like Claire, for instance. Yesterday all I cared about was making sure that she thought Robby was cool enough to be my stepbrother. Today, it doesn't worry me one iota. Yesterday I thought adults got everything right all of the time. Today I think not.

'Can you and Robby give me a hand, please?' Sue's voice brought me back to the here and now. 'I want to put these two tables together . . .'

Robby and I did as we were told.

'Right, can you lay it up for seven, please? We've got a reservation for a late lunch today.'

'Wow! Like a posh restaurant, Sue!' I joked.

'What do you mean? We *are* a posh restaurant!'

I was getting serviettes from the counter and watching Robby putting out the cutlery. It was weird but it was as though I'd only just been told that he was my stepbrother. I mean, I'd known for years that I'd got this stepbrother in Scotland who was three years older than me, and I'd known for days that it was Robby. But it was only right now, this minute, that I actually took it in properly.

On our walk together the previous evening, I'd asked him what he was going to do now.

'Stay here for the rest of the summer. And after that, I don't know. I'd quite like the chance to go back to Scotland and tell Mum and my stepdad where they can shove their private education.'

'And then what?'

'Dunno. Depends on their reaction.'

I went into the kitchen at the sound of Adrian's little bell and picked up the order for table two. Robby was washing up now. Even the sight of his back made me feel sad. I hoped he wouldn't go back to Scotland. I'd only just got to know him.

This morning when I'd come into the café he'd already been hard at work, and he'd looked so happy to see me. I'd started quizzing him on what had happened when Mum and Colin had got back the previous evening.

'I was in my room,' he said, 'and they left me alone. Then this morning I got up at the last minute. I saw Kathy on the landing and she said, "Morning, Alisdair," as though nothing had happened. I didn't see Dad, thank God. But what happened at your place?'

'Jon was in bed when I got back. He looked like he'd been crying so I sat with him for ages and kept telling him it wasn't his fault. He said the adults had been shouting and Anne had sent him up for a bath. After I'd left Jon I went into my own room and listened to music until it was bed time. Anne came in and gave me a kiss, but I pretended to be asleep.'

After that Robby and I didn't have time for any conversation except little snippets here and there. By quarter to two, though, the place was much less crowded.

Sue followed me into the kitchen.

'What time is the reservation for, Sue?'

'Two o'clock. Why don't you have a quick break while it's quiet.'

Robby came in with a tray piled high with cups, saucers and glasses. He started loading them into the dishwasher.

'I'll help you, Robby. I don't feel like a break.'

There were loads of things I wanted to talk to Robby about, but I decided to wait till we were on our own.

A few minutes later we were both heading out of the kitchen to see if the late lunch party had arrived, when Adrian stopped us. 'Sorry, guys, I've got a few pans and things that need washing.'

So Robby washed and I wiped.

Then Sue came in. 'Could you two come in to the café,' she said.

There were still quite a few pans left. 'It's OK, I'll go,' I whispered to Robby. 'You finish these off.'

'Actually, I'll need you both,' said Sue.

Robby and I glanced at Adrian.

He shrugged, then grinned, 'She's the boss!'

Then into the kitchen walked Mandy, the waitress who had a particularly soft spot for me, because I'd knocked her lemonade over. What was *she* doing here?

Robby was looking as puzzled as I was.

'Just go!' said Adrian, grinning.

So Robby and I followed Sue out into the café, but a moment later we nearly bolted straight back into the kitchen, because sitting at the table for seven were Mum, Colin, Anne, Dad and Jon.

'And these last two places are for you two,' smiled Sue. 'Mandy, would you go and get the champagne from the fridge, please?'

I seemed to be rooted to the spot. So did Robby.

Colin stood up and spoke quietly. 'This is our attempt at an apology,' he said, looking straight at Robby. 'We had a long talk last night, Kathy and I, and now . . .'

'Now we want to listen,' Mum finished off.

'There's a lot to talk about, –' *Please don't mention exams or university!* – 'like what you want to do with all those brilliant photos, for a start!'

Robby went pink, and I thought back to that first time I saw him in here. What a lot had happened since then!

'Sit down, you two. I'm starving,' said Jon.

'Yes, *please* sit down, Bethany,' Mandy said, giving me a knowing look. 'I'm about to hand round these full glasses!'

I laughed as I sat down next to Anne, with Robby on the other side of me.

Anne squeezed my hand. 'I'm so proud of you,' she whispered. 'It must have taken a lot of guts to keep Alisdair's secret.'

'Actually,' I whispered back, 'do you mind if we call him Robby from now on?'

Mum overheard me saying that. 'Please raise your glasses,' she said. Everyone did as they were told. 'Not you,' she said to Robby. He cracked into his first smile since we'd come out of the kitchen when she said that. 'To Robby!' said Mum.

'To Robby!' everyone repeated.

'Quick! Raise them again before Jon drinks the lot!' said Robby. Then he looked at me. 'And here's to my sister, Bethany.'

'To Bethany!' everyone said.

I felt really special at that moment. And then I felt gobsmacked, because Mum leaned forwards. 'A little present, darling . . .'

In her hand was a pair of the coolest dangly earrings. I went bright red and my hands shot to my ears.

'I'm not blind!' she said, giving me a pretend strict look.

'Thanks, Mum,' I laughed.

'I think we need a top-up,' said Colin, holding up his glass.

'I'll do it,' said Robby and I, leaping to our feet at the same moment.

Everyone laughed, and Robby and I exchanged a look that was too full of stuff to explain. But I think the general gist of it was that we knew there was still a lot to sort out, but everything was going to be easier now, because we were a great team, he and I.

A great brother and sister team.

Step-Chain

LOSING MY IDENTITY

1 JOSS'S FAN CLUB

Thank God it's Sunday night!

I'm sitting up in bed, reading a comic, only I can't concentrate because of thinking of all that's happened since yesterday morning. When I look at the empty space on the floor between the bed and the window, I get this really good feeling. I get it every other weekend at exactly this time.

Thirteen whole nights with no Joss sleeping on my floor.

Thirteen whole nights! I wish it was thirteen whole years – then I'd be twenty-six and I'd be able to do exactly what I wanted, without him making my life a misery. If he bugged me I'd just say, *Get lost, Joss!*

So why I can't I say it now?

'Get lost, Joss!'

I feel a right idiot sitting here in bed, saying it out loud to an empty room. Then I get this horrible nervous feeling. What if it *isn't* empty? What if Joss is still here? Hiding under the bed, creased up laughing. He can't be. It's daft. I know that.

But I still get out of bed and check. It makes me sick. He controls me even when he's not here. But it's a million times worse when he *is* here. I kind of have to do what he says. Because if I don't, he'll make me suffer.

It's only me. He doesn't pick on anyone else.

Like this weekend, for example . . . This is what happened.

* * *

On Saturday morning the doorbell rings and I'm sitting at the top of the stairs. Mum and Mark go to answer it together, like some kind of welcoming committee.

'Hello, Joss love,' says Mum. 'Come in, come in!'

'Hello, son,' says Mark. And even though I can't see properly, I know he's giving Joss the usual greeting, which is half way between a pat on the back and a hug.

I come down a couple of steps and watch Mum and Mark's quick wave and false smile. That's for Joanna's benefit. She's in the car. Then they shut the door and call out to me. It happens like this every other weekend when Joss comes here to visit Mark – *his* dad, *my* stepdad.

'There you are, Ryan!' says Mum.

'Hi!' I call out, trying to sound cool. This time I'm really going to show him that things have changed round here, and he isn't going to boss me around any more. (I say that to myself every time he comes, but it never works.)

'Hiya, Titch!'

Mum and Mark smile. It makes me sick the way they think Joss and I are best mates. I've even heard Mum telling her friends on the phone that it's 'super' the way the two boys are so close – almost like real brothers. 'It's sweet,' she says in her mumsy voice, 'Joss calls Ryan Titch as a sort of affectionate nickname!' I want to scream at her, 'No he doesn't! He calls me Titch because he once came in when I was in the bath, and burst out laughing and said he'd never seen such a weedy little thirteen year old.'

Actually he only calls me Titch when Mum and Mark are around. The rest of the time he calls me Weedo.

But that'll soon stop, once he sees I'm not going to put up with it any more.

Mum looks a bit puzzled. 'Are you coming down, Ryan?'

'Yep.'

Right, this is it . . .

I've been practising this cool *coming downstairs technique* for days. It's definitely going to impress Joss, this. It only works if I'm wearing my red sweatshirt, which is made of smooth stuff. I have to lean to one side, so the top of my arm's against the banister with all my weight behind it. Then, because of my slippery sweatshirt, I start sliding down, and the very second that happens I have to run really fast, to make sure the bottom half of my body follows just behind. I tell you, it takes massive co-ordination.

Trouble is, by the time I've got myself in position, Joss is already following Mum to the kitchen.

'Hey, Joss!' I call.

But I'm leaning too far forwards, 'cos I'm so

keen to get on with it. And there's no way my feet can keep up. I fall forwards, make a grab for the railings, miss, and land in a heap at the bottom of the stairs.

'Oooops!'

Mum's bending over me, so I can't see the look on Joss's face. 'Are you all right, darling?'

My chin, my shoulder and my bum are all hurting like mad, but there's no way Joss is going to know that. 'Yeah, I just . . . slipped.'

I roll over to my hands and knees and I'm about to get up when my three-year-old sister appears and clambers on to my back. 'Come on, horsey!' she cries. 'Gee up!'

'Get off, Rosie!'

'OK, grumpy gee gee!' She giggles as she slides off.

I straighten up and Mum kisses me, which makes me feel a right baby. 'I think you've got a touch of topplitis!' she chuckles.

I distinctly hear Joss snigger before he strolls off.

Great start!

'Bad luck,' says Mark, grinning at me, which makes me go red.

'Come and have a muffin, Ryan,' says Rosie, grabbing my hand.

Yeah, that'll make everything OK, ha ha!

After dinner Mum goes out into the back garden to peg the washing out. I follow her. I want to talk to her without Joss hearing. It's pathetic, I know, but I've already given up on the *Keep cool, act tough, sweat it out* plan, and no way am I about to stay in this house with Joss.

'I'll come shopping with you I think, Mum.'

'We can't leave Joss on his own when he only comes here once a fortnight, can we, hm?'

This is *not* what I want to hear.

'But he comes to see Mark, not me. How

about I help you with the shopping, and Mark stays here with Joss?'

Mum stops hanging things up and turns a big beam on me. 'That's sweet of you, darling, but it's not just food shopping we're going to do, it's –' She giggles. '– it's alternative shopping!'

Oh great! Mum's off to buy a load of oil and incense and candles and all that kind of hippy stuff. It's so embarrassing having such a weird mother. I'm sure Mark thinks she's a bit of a freak, but he's in love with her, isn't he, so he can't see how bad it is.

'Why can't you do that on your own, Mum?'

'Do what?' Joss is standing at the back door.

I kick the grass and feel gutted. Now Mum'll tell Joss, then I'll get the rip taken out of me all afternoon.

'Mark and I are off to the aromatherapy place this afternoon . . .'

'Great. Ryan and me'll stay here.'

Mum's eyes go all shiny and gooey. She thinks the sun shines out of Joss's bum. That's because he's always nice and polite to her. Well, let's face it, he's nice and polite to everyone – except me. 'Why don't you ask Dan or Mitch to come round, Ryan?' She puts the last peg in and laughs brightly. 'Or both of them!'

'No, it's OK . . .'

'Why not, Titch?'

Because I don't want my best mates to meet you. You'll put on a big act and find a way to turn them against me. That's why.

'They're both going out today. They told me at school.'

I'm trying to look normal but I know Joss can tell I'm lying. 'Let's just ring and check, eh? It's about time I met a few of your mates, Titch!'

Mum smiles and rushes off indoors. 'Better still, I'll give their mums a ring.'

I dig my heel into the lawn and grind it round a bit.

'Temper, temper!' says Joss under his breath. 'Don't you want your friends to meet your brother?' I hate it when he calls himself my brother.

'Don't care,' I mumble, following Mum inside.

Dan and Mitch turn up about half an hour later. Mum, Mark and Rosie go out just afterwards.

'Be good!' Mum calls upstairs in her jokey way. (Dead funny, yeah.)

'Yes, be good little boys!' Rosie yells out in her silliest voice just before the front door closes behind them all.

We're all sitting round in my room. It feels awkward with Joss here. He pulls some chewing gum out of his pocket. 'Want some, you guys?'

Mitch and Dan take a piece each. 'Want some, Rye?'

I shake my head. It's starting already. He's being the nice guy. Calling me Rye, not Weedo.

'What shall we do?' I ask, trying not to sound too grumpy.

'Do you know how to play coin rugby?' Joss asks.

'I've heard of it,' says Dan.

'Me too,' Mitch says.

I haven't, but I say I have, and we go down to the kitchen.

'OK, we need a two-pence piece . . .' Joss pulls open the top drawer of the dresser and takes a coin from mum's 'rainy day box' as she calls it. (I didn't know he even knew about the box.) He leans over the breakfast counter. 'This surface is perfect. You get that side, Mitch. Only two can play at once.'

Then he explains the rules. It's all to do with

sliding the coin exactly the right distance, then flipping it, catching it, spinning it and chucking it from between your two thumbs.

'Whoever wins gets to play the next person, OK?'

Clever rule that, because guess who keeps winning? Dan and Mitch go on and on about how wicked coin rugby is, and how they're going to show everyone at school. It's obvious they're impressed with Joss.

I'm the last one to play him. I'm usually rubbish at all sports, even games like this, but by some fluke I do really well. I even manage to do a whole 'run'.

The last bit is best because I send the coin sailing right up in the air and it hits him on the chest. 'Yesss! Seven points to me. That puts me in the lead, yeah?'

'No it doesn't.'

I might have guessed . . . 'What do you mean?'

'There's a rule that if you hit the opponent, you lose all your points. Bad luck, Rye.'

Mitch and Dan laugh. 'Yeah, bad luck, Giggsy.' (That's them taking the rip about me being useless at sport.) The big wind up is starting. I sit down at the kitchen table because I feel so hacked off. So now Mitch and Dan think I'm sulking, don't they? This is what Joss does. Subtle stuff. Drip drip.

'Uh-oh!' he says, grinning at Mitch and Dan. 'Think we'd better do something else, guys! We can't have old Titch in a sweat.' They laugh. It makes me sick. 'Anyone want to come into town?'

'Yeah!' says the fan club of two.